Lure of the Wolf

Aloha Shifters: Jewels of the Heart

by Anna Lowe

Editing by Lisa A. Hollett

Covert art by Kim Killion

Contents

Contents   i

Other books in this series   iii

Free Books   183

Chapter One   1

Chapter Two   7

Chapter Three   15

Chapter Four   25

Chapter Five   35

Chapter Six   45

Chapter Seven   55

Chapter Eight   65

Chapter Nine   73

Chapter Ten   83

Chapter Eleven   91

Chapter Twelve   99

Chapter Thirteen   109

Chapter Fourteen   117

Chapter Fifteen   127

Chapter Sixteen   135

Chapter Seventeen   145

Chapter Eighteen   157

Chapter Nineteen   163

Sneak Peek: Lure of the Bear   173

Books by Anna Lowe   179

Free Books   183

About the Author   185

Other books in this series

Aloha Shifters - Jewels of the Heart

Lure of the Dragon (Book 1)

Lure of the Wolf (Book 2)

Lure of the Bear (Book 3)

Lure of the Tiger (Book 4)

Love of the Dragon (Book 5)

visit www.annalowebooks.com

Free Books

Get your free e-books now!

Sign up for my newsletter at *annalowebooks.com* to get three free books!

- *Desert Wolf*: Friend or Foe (Book 1.1 in the Twin Moon Ranch series)

- *Off the Charts* (the prequel to the Serendipity Adventure series)

- *Perfection* (the prequel to the Blue Moon Saloon series)

Chapter One

"No!"

Nina screamed and flailed, but that didn't stop the thick arms that grappled with her.

"Finish her off already," one man barked as she was flung across a narrow space.

Her head thumped against something hard, and she slumped to the ground. Everything went dim as the voices closed in around her.

"Is she dead?" Someone prodded her shoulder.

Her head spun from the blow, and bile rose in her throat. Where was she? What was happening? How had she gotten to this dark, wet place?

"She's still breathing," a man said above the ringing in her ears. He was close enough to engulf her with his vile breath, but she couldn't move.

"Well, she won't be alive much longer. I need her dead. But it needs to look like an accident," the first man said in a strangely familiar voice. Moments ago, she'd recognized him. Now, nothing made sense. The blow to her head had rattled her memories around. Nothing fit into place.

"Accidental drowning, if they find her body at all. Come on. You get her feet," the second man said, and they lifted her.

She flexed her fingers and moaned.

"On three," the man said, swinging her body through the air.

She already felt sick, but the motion only made things worse. She blinked, desperate to pull herself together before it was too late.

"Two. . ."

A gnawing sense of dread spread through her bones. Why were her limbs so slow to react? Why was she so confused?

"Three," the man grunted, and she was airborne.

She flailed helplessly before hitting the water, closing her mouth too late. Salt water choked her, and an invisible weight yanked her body into the depths of the Pacific. Terror gripped her — enough to jolt her halfway to her senses. She kicked toward the moonlight, desperate for air.

When she broke through the surface, gulping wildly, her long brown hair covered her face. She pushed at the tangles and coughed so hard it hurt.

"Wait! Help!" she managed to scream.

A bad idea — attracting the attention of the men who'd just thrown her off a boat. They wanted her dead, but she couldn't quite process that thought. Why would anyone want to kill her? What had she done?

"Shit, she's not dead," one of the men grunted.

"Not yet, she isn't," the other replied.

Bang! Something flat and solid smashed the water right beside her head.

Move it, fast! a voice in the back of her mind cried. Those men were swatting at her with an oar — and aiming for her head. *They want you dead. Get away!*

She paddled frantically. How was she supposed to get away? The lights that dotted the shoreline — Maui's shoreline; that much she knew — were faint and distant. The only boat in sight was the sleek white motor yacht she'd just been shoved off. *Angel's* something — she could see the name embossed across the stern in gold.

She kicked backward as the oar hit the water again and again, thrusting at her like a club. It glanced off her arm, and she choked in pain.

"Hurry up," one man urged the other.

The oar slammed into her shoulder. It grazed the side of her head when they pulled it back, and her vision blurred.

"Get her!" she heard the man yell again, but his voice was distant and fading away.

If you black out now, you will die, the inner voice screamed. *Dive! Now! Go!*

Nina didn't dive so much as sink. The water muffled all sound, and salt stung in her eyes. Which way was up? Which way was down?

Moonlight filtered through the water, and though instinct told her to kick toward it, she paddled sideways before surfacing again. The breath she inhaled drew in as much water as air, and she sputtered wildly.

"She's over there!" one of the men shouted.

She wanted to scream, to cry. There had to be some mistake. But she could barely breathe, let alone speak, so all she managed was a garbled moan.

"Forget it," the other muttered. "No way will she make it all the way to shore. We're three miles out."

He was right, and she knew it. The ocean was relatively still, but land was miles away. Her clothes were soaked, her limbs stiff. Her head throbbed, and her vision was blurry.

Do something! Now! instinct screamed as the motorboat powered up and sped away.

She yanked one shoe off, then the other. Her legs kept tangling in her skirt, so she shed that, too, and let the ocean swallow the fabric up.

The ocean will swallow you too, if you don't get moving. Go!

She turned in a slow circle, wondering which way to go. Wondering why she even bothered. Maybe she should let death take her quickly instead of fighting it.

You're not a quitter. You can't be. Just like Mom. She wasn't a quitter.

Nina sobbed at the thought of her mother. So sick, so frail, yet refusing to give up the fight. That single memory was clear in the foggy landscape of her mind.

Come on, make her proud.

She slapped the water, as if the ocean were to blame for the cancer that had stolen her mother away. Then the sound of the motorboat's engine changed, and she spun around, seeing it turn back.

"Finish her off!" the man shouted.

The engine revved to a roar, and the boat accelerated, kicking a plume of water in its wake as it sliced through the water, heading her way.

"No!"

She couldn't see into the deckhouse, but she could imagine two men hunched over the controls, grinning madly.

Move! Swim! Now!

Frantically, she paddled right. The engine throbbed, filling the air and the water with its brute force. The water around her lifted with the bow wave, and she swam for her life, high on a sudden rush of adrenaline.

Faster! Go! Go!

Water frothed all around her, making her tumble and turn as if caught in a breaker off a beach. There was a deafening hiss, a hammering throb. The terrifying sense of a mighty hulk slicing the water behind her.

And, *zoom!* The motor yacht zipped past. Nina bobbed to the surface just in time to see the bow carve through the water an arm's length away. She kicked backward, desperate to clear the propellers, hacking and coughing the whole time.

Alive. She was alive. Her lungs cried, and her body ached, but she was alive. She heaved and sputtered, watching the yacht buzz toward the distant shore.

She treaded water, trying to catch her breath — and to make sense of it all. But her mind was hazy, and her memories were a jumbled mess. Where was she? What happened?

The loose shirt she'd been wearing floated around her, restricting her arms, so she pulled it over her head and cast it aside. Floating was easier without it, but still, it was an awfully long way to land.

So swim. Just swim. One easy stroke after another.

She wanted to protest, but her arms were already obeying the inner command, as if that were her mother begging her.

Don't think, honey. Just swim.

The moon rippled over the water. The hum of the yacht's engine faded away, and an eerie peace settled over the ocean.

Swim, honey. The way you used to go all the way across the lake.

That lake, wherever it was, was little more than a faint memory. And heck, this was no lake.

You can do this. One stroke at a time.

The ocean rose and fell with the long, lazy rhythm of the swell, and she imagined that it was cheering for her, too.

You can do it. One stroke at a time.

Chapter Two

Nina had no idea how long she swam or how far. She simply swam, looking up from time to time. The lights didn't seem to grow any brighter or nearer, but strangely, she didn't despair. Her body was on autopilot, swimming weakly along, and she let her mind tune out. Maybe drowning wouldn't be as bad if her mind was as numb as her fingertips.

She switched to her back at some point and looked up at the twinkling stars. Maybe they were rooting for her. Maybe she'd make it after all.

She lost track of everything and faded into a trance that may or may not have been death grasping at her toes. One minute, she was dreaming about dolphins, and the next, her hand closed over coarse, gritty sand. She kicked feebly, wondering why she wasn't moving any more, then closed her eyes. Let death take her. She didn't care any more.

"Hey!" A deep voice reached her groggy mind.

A wave swished over sand, and she flexed her fingers. Sand? She blinked. It was still night, but darker than before — so late, the moon had set. Pebbly bits of coral jutted into her belly, and her head ached. Her shoulder, too.

"Hey, you can't be here," the man said again. His deep, resounding voice stroked her skin and warmed her threadbare nerves.

She lifted her head, blinking, but dropped it back to the sand a second later. Just that small movement made her head swim.

She wanted to say something like, *I'll be out of here as soon as I can lift more than a finger,* but all that came out was a groan.

Two bare feet lined up inches from her face, and the man spoke again, more quietly this time.

"Lady, are you okay?"

She laughed, which came out as a cackling kind of moan. No, she was not okay. Not by a long shot.

"I hate to say it, but this is private property. No trespassing. Which means..."

She let his voice fade away. What did it matter if she trespassed? She was alive.

He touched her shoulder, and she hummed. In light of what had just transpired, she ought to have panicked at being so close to a stranger, but all she felt was warmth and hope. As if her mother were coming to take care of her and everything would be okay.

The man turned her gently, and a warm hand touched her aching brow.

"Jesus, what happened?"

Funny, she wanted to ask the same thing.

She tipped her head back. God, he smelled good. Or did the whole beach smell like sandalwood and Old Spice?

"Can you hear me?" he asked, kneeling over her.

She tried to nod, but couldn't. Her nerve endings were firing blanks, and she was tired. So, so tired.

"Does this hurt?" he asked, touching her arm.

It had until he touched it. Then all she felt was a cozy, enveloping heat. A sense of security.

"Hang on," he whispered, sliding his hands under her body.

She held her breath, wondering if her nightmare was about to get worse.

"Don't hurt me," she said, curling up into a ball.

"I won't hurt you," he whispered.

"Promise," she insisted, though her voice was weak. It was childish, really, because he could break his promise. Men did that all the time.

He paused for what seemed like an awfully long time, and panic crept in toward her again. Was he going to hurt her? Rape her? Smash her over the head?

"I promise I won't hurt you." His voice was soft. Impossibly soft and kind. "Okay?"

"Okay," she mumbled like a sleepy child — or a woman about to pass out.

Her senses had been drifting in and out, but the second he cradled her against his chest, she felt wide awake.

She looked up and blinked into his eyes. Pure, indigo eyes that glowed and flared like hot coals, framed by the rugged features of the world's most handsome man. Which had to mean she was hallucinating — but heck, hallucinating was better than facing the ugly truth. Maybe she'd go with it a little longer. She'd pretend that this was her dream man coming to her rescue and not some hairy old hermit or whoever it was. Because no real man had ever looked at her with eyes so gentle and so concerned — not one with that much muscle, anyway.

"Hang on. You'll be okay."

Palms whispered overhead as he strode along, and the fragrance of hibiscus mixed with his earthy scent. Crickets sang from the lush foliage, and a bird called. Maybe she'd died and gone to heaven, and this man was an angel carrying her toward the pearly gates.

"You'll be okay," he repeated, covering her with something soft and clean. A blanket? No, a beach towel he'd grabbed off a railing as he walked. She clutched at a corner of the fabric. God, she really ought to get herself out of baby-in-the-womb mode, but she just couldn't find the energy.

She stared, focusing on his eyes. Either the indigo had brightened to a royal blue, or she'd been imagining things. His sandy hair feathered and curled to a point just below his ears. As he walked, he glanced down, checking on her. It should have been awkward, being face-to-face with a perfect stranger, but it simply felt right. So, so right.

The cadence of his steps changed slightly; he was going uphill. The rolling sound of breakers faded, replaced by a gurgling stream, and the air was filled with a scent of ginger. Somewhere ahead, a light shone.

"Almost there," he murmured.

9

Almost where? She tightened her grip on his thick forearm and blinked at a dim point of light.

The hum of voices carried on the wind as he walked on, and the light grew brighter.

She wished her legs would obey her order to stretch and slide to the ground, but they wouldn't. He was carrying her over to a group of people. A group of men, from the sound of it, not far ahead.

"Don't worry," her knight whispered in her ear.

Which reassured her for exactly one second until he stepped into the circle of light.

"Whoa," another man said, and a chair scraped over a tile floor.

"Holy..." another exclaimed.

"What the hell?" a third growled, and Nina immediately tensed. She wasn't welcome here. God, she was at the mercy of these men. They could do anything—

"Shh," her knight reassured her, tilting his arms to let her snuggle closer to his chest. She closed her eyes and breathed him in, letting his breezy, salt-air scent calm her.

He leaned down and placed her gently on what felt like the world's softest couch. When he slid his arms out from under her, a wave of sorrow washed over her. She'd never felt more alone or more vulnerable. But then he brushed a hand along her cheek and whispered, and her nerves calmed a little bit.

"Shh. You'll be okay. I promise." His tone practically chiseled the words into stone.

She managed a tiny nod, but her eyes remained sealed tight. She didn't have the energy or the nerve to open them just yet. The voices were frightening enough.

"What happened?" a deep, rumbly voice demanded.

"Get that light out of her eyes," her knight barked, his voice suddenly harsher, harder.

"What the hell are you doing, bringing a human in here like this?" another asked.

Nina shook her head a little. Did someone just say human, or was that the ringing in her ears?

"Jesus, Boone. What's going on?"

10

She'd been fading out again, but at the mention of his name, she perked up a little. Boone. Was her rescuer named Boone?

"We need to find Silas," the one with the deep, growly voice said.

"No, don't!" Boone barked.

Nina cringed, almost wishing she'd black out again. Was Silas a bad man? Bad like the men she'd escaped earlier that night?

Wait. What men had she escaped? She shook her head a little, but the memories escaped as quickly as they'd flitted through her mind.

"We don't need Silas," Boone said.

"What happened?" someone asked, leaning in.

Her eyes fluttered open, and she blinked. Three men came into focus, all of them looming over her. Big, burly men with inscrutable faces and searching eyes. She shrank back and clutched at the beach towel covering her body. All she had on after shedding her clothing in the water was a string bikini top and a skimpy bottom. Her skin itched from the crust of dried salt — and from the scrutiny.

They were in an open-sided shelter of some kind — a big, open space set up like a living room. Make that a man-den. A clubhouse, almost, with deep couches and a bar to one side, open to the fresh sea breeze and covered with a thatched palm roof.

"You're okay now," the nearest man murmured, and her eyes jumped to him.

Him. Boone. Her rescuer, who wasn't a hairy hermit, after all, nor a mountain god as she'd half suspected when he'd carried her so effortlessly. He was a sandy-haired, athletic man who took her breath away. His eyebrows curved up when he looked at her, and he nodded as if to agree with everything she had to say. His skin was a toned copper color, and his eyes—

The second the boundless blue of his eyes met hers, her pulse skipped.

"Hey," he whispered. "It will be all right."

11

That made her feel better, but when the other two men started lobbing questions at her, she wavered again. Everything was a haze.

"What happened?"

Something bad. Something she'd rather not remember. She touched her head and immediately winced.

"What are you doing here?"

God, she wished she knew.

Boone shouldered a tall, dark-haired man aside, sheltering her from the onslaught.

"What's your name?" he asked, so quietly, so gently, she wanted to cry.

Then she really did cry, because she couldn't remember. The *Nina* part came out automatically, but after that, she got stuck. Nina... Nina who? She searched her memories and found them horrifyingly blank, like a photo negative left too long in the sun.

"Where are you staying?"

"Who can we call?"

"How did you get here?"

The questions surrounded her like a swarm of hornets, and no matter how she tried, she couldn't find an answer to any of them. The harder she searched her mind, the more frantic she became. Like a person who'd lost the most precious thing imaginable, she searched the pockets of her mind, one after another and then all over again.

Her mouth opened and closed, but still, no words came. No memories, either.

A boat... two men... shouts...

But she didn't remember stepping foot on a boat. She didn't remember anything up to the moment she'd been thrown overboard. "Two men... threw me... A boat..." she murmured, but her words were as disjointed as her thoughts.

"What boat? What men?" someone demanded.

She threw her hands over her face and rolled sideways, trying to hide the tears, wishing she could disappear into the couch — as if she still had a scrap of pride to protect.

"Back off," Boone barked, and just like that, the hubbub ceased. His voice was so sharp, so commanding, even she peeked up.

The other men looked startled at the command. They were equals, she sensed, unused to taking orders from each other. Any one of them could have led an elite military platoon, judging by the hard lines of their faces and their wide, no-nonsense stances. But for that moment, at least, Boone outranked them all.

"Back off," he murmured again, and they did.

He readjusted the towel over her body and patted her arm. *It will be okay,* the gesture said. *I swear it will be okay.*

She closed her eyes and focused on his touch — the only thing keeping her from going over the edge there and then.

"Get me that dish towel," he murmured. A moment later, he wiped her face with a moist cloth. Slowly. Carefully. Tenderly, almost.

"She fell off a boat?" one of the men asked in a hushed voice that the others matched.

"Got pushed off, from the sounds of it," another one corrected.

She wished they would all be quiet and let her pretend Boone was the only one in the room.

"Why would someone push her overboard?"

"Because they want her dead."

"Why? What did she do?"

Nina wasn't looking, but she felt their inquisitive glances bore into her skin.

"Why can't she remember anything?"

She screamed at herself in her mind, wondering the same thing.

"Shock. Fear. Bump on the head?" Someone went through a whole catalog of possibilities. And damn, every one was true.

"So what are you going to do?" one of them asked Boone.

A heavy silence followed, and Nina held her breath. His hand brushed hers uncertainly.

Help me, she wanted to scream. *Please help me.*

"Let her rest," he said at length. "Maybe she'll remember after she gets some rest."

Rest sounded good. Her body begged for it, and her mind latched on to the idea. All she needed was some rest, and everything would come back again, right?

"We have to tell Silas," someone said.

Nina went tense all over. Whoever Silas was, she already knew to steer clear of him.

"Later," Boone growled. "I'll tell him soon. First, I have to take care of her."

Taking care of had so many meanings, but she concentrated on the positive ones. Like the image of Boone tucking her into a bed and promising everything would be okay.

"Hang on," he murmured, picking her up again.

She mumbled a halfhearted protest but immediately melted into place against him. Her chest against his, her arms around his neck. It all came naturally, just the way his arms fitted around her shoulders and knees.

"All you need is some sleep," he assured her as he walked. "Everything will be okay."

He carried her back toward the beach, and before she knew it, he was tucking her into a huge, cozy bed. She slipped in like Goldilocks going right for the biggest bed and hugged a pillow tightly, wondering if she could ever get to sleep.

A weight settled on the mattress behind her as he sat, stroking her shoulder.

"It will be okay," he whispered.

Her eyelids drooped. Her body practically sighed. She'd gone from lost and terrified to safe and totally secure. A moment later, she dropped off into a blissfully dreamless sleep.

Chapter Three

Boone took a deep breath and ordered himself to back up toward the door.

Just one more second, his inner wolf breathed.

He didn't need a second. He needed to get the hell out before his wolf got any bad ideas — like memorizing the soft lines of her face and the gentle curves of her body. Like sniffing her closely and inhaling her heavenly scent. The scent that screamed at him, *Mate, mate!*

He backed away slowly, shaking his head. Maybe he'd gone too long without a woman's company. Maybe his wolf was just totally fucked up. There was no way this human could be his mate.

She's beautiful, his wolf murmured, watching her sleep.

He tried tearing his eyes away. Yes, she was beautiful, even in her disheveled state. Not runway-model-beautiful, but genuine, hometown, girl-next-door beautiful. The kind who didn't need makeup or fancy clothes to stand out in a crowd. The kind who shone from the inside out.

He slammed on his mental brakes. Okay, okay. So she was pretty. So what?

She's in danger. She needs our help, his wolf insisted.

His heart pounded harder at the thought of the bump on her head. Someone had tried to kill her. But why? Who?

His wolf rumbled in anger. *Someone we will find and tear to pieces very, very soon.*

Boone shook his head. He wasn't going to get involved. He was getting the hell out of his cottage before she opened her eyes and saw him in the state he was in. His eyes were glowing — he could feel the heat behind them — and his fangs were ready to extend. His inner wolf was close to the surface, angry and aroused. Absolutely sure this woman was the one.

Mate. She is my destined mate, his wolf chanted, again and again.

Boone shook his head bitterly. *That's what you said about Tammy.*

This is different, his wolf insisted.

It did feel different. His heart had never skipped so hard or fast, and his stomach was full of butterflies. Tammy had made him laugh — and cry — but the reaction was never as visceral, as intense.

This time I'm sure, his wolf said.

He snorted. *I'll take that as proof of how wrong you are.*

His wolf had been sure about Tammy, once upon a time. His human side, too. He'd never met anyone who moved him to such levels of passion — or pain.

I love you, too, Boone. I'll wait for you as long as it takes, Tammy had said. And yet she'd broken every heartfelt promise she'd made when he deployed.

Boone clenched his jaw. Tammy had broken his heart — make that, smashed it to bits with a wrecking ball. Which meant that the whole notion of destined mates was nonsense. Old-timers still believed in the legends, but no self-respecting wolf shifter believed in fate any more. Not these days.

He shook his head. He'd learned that lesson the hard way, and he wasn't about to lose his heart — or head — again.

Except, shit. This mystery woman called to his soul, and he'd just tucked her into his bed. Worse, he'd promised her everything would be okay. Years ago, he'd sworn off promising anything to anyone, except maybe promising his brothers-in-arms that he'd guard their backs the way they guarded his. How the hell was he going to make sure she was okay without getting involved?

He glanced back one more time — bad idea, because a wisp of brown hair had fallen over her face, and he longed to smooth it out of the way — then dragged himself out the back in a rush. He shut the door behind him and leaned against it as if there were a wolf on the inside trying to get out instead of a wolf in *his* inside begging to rush back in. When he glanced up, his eyes landed on the curving line of a constellation. Scorpio. If that wasn't a sign for him to tread carefully, what was?

Forget about Scorpio. The ancient Hawaiians called it Maui's hook, his wolf huffed. *The hook the god used to haul these islands out of the sea.*

Yeah, well. He was still going to watch out for trouble. Now that he'd gone and promised, he'd see that vow through. He cast a glance over his shoulder at his own weather-beaten bungalow. A second later, he winced. Here he was, a full-grown man, still living in what was little more than a shack on the beach. He barely had three digits in his bank account. Even if the beautiful stranger was his mate, what did he have to offer other than a couple of surfboards and the battered treasures he'd found on the beach?

We do have the best view on Maui, his wolf tried, not quite getting the point.

Boone sighed, watching the moonlight dance over the sea. Great. He had a view and not much to show for three decades of existence except for a lot of scars — inside and out.

"Heya," a low voice called.

Boone whipped around then relaxed. It was Hunter, the sole bear in their band of shifter-soldiers doing their best to live quiet, honest lives on Maui's untamed northwest shores.

"She okay?" the grizzly asked, jerking his head toward the bungalow.

Boone nodded. "For now, I guess."

Hunter tilted his head, paused for an eternity — bears took forever to put their thoughts into words — and finally spoke. "What about you?"

Boone wanted to laugh and say something like, *Of course. Why wouldn't I be okay?* But damn, his pulse was still racing, his skin still tingling from the woman's touch.

Nina. Her name is Nina, his wolf said.

He wanted to jam his hands over his ears, but what good would that do? His wolf was a goner. He had to rely on his more rational human half if he was going to resist the inexplicable pull to the woman in his bed.

"I'm fine. Perfect."

Hunter let that one slide. "Silas is back. You gotta tell him, you know."

Boone went perfectly still for a moment, then told himself to relax. Okay, so Silas was back from whatever black-tie event he'd been at. No problem, right?

Still, he took a deep breath and kicked the dirt before looking up toward the mansion built into the hill like an eagle's nest. They were all equals here — he and the other shifters who'd settled on Koa Point. He was the only wolf; Hunter, the sole bear; and Cruz, the only tiger in a ragtag bunch that had been whipped into an elite military corps through a lot of blood, sweat, and tears. Despite their differences, they'd bonded into a band of brothers through many trials by fire. Every man had his strengths and a few carefully concealed weaknesses, and no one stood out above the rest.

Except Silas, the dragon shifter he had to face right now. Silas had been the leader of their top-secret Special Forces unit, and under him, a gang of stubborn individuals had become the perfect team, all dedicated to serving their country in covert overseas ops. Now that they were civilians again, Silas wasn't anyone's superior — technically speaking, at least. But old habits died hard, and everyone still treated the dragon as top dog. Silas was also the one who'd reunited the men a few months after they'd left the military and gone their separate ways — months in which every one of them had struggled for orientation until Silas invited them to this idyllic Hawaiian hideaway.

Here's the plan, Silas had said. *I got us the caretaker's contract at an amazing estate. We'll form an exclusive private investigator/bodyguard agency. We'll pick and choose the cases we take. Earn good money. Live the good life. Maybe even watch the sun set from time to time — or whatever it is that civilians do.*

They'd all laughed at that, even though that had been the crux of the problem with their transition to civilian life. What exactly would they all do next? Few of them had families or

18

packs to return to. None really had a plan beyond retiring from wars that had stolen far too many innocent lives.

Silas had the plan, the connections, and clients lined up from the word *go*, and they'd all signed on. The work provided just enough of that feeling of living on the edge that they all missed. On the whole, though, life was easy — maybe too easy, Boone reflected — and everyone had his own space while they still had each other. A band of brothers who understood one another better than any outsider ever could.

His mind jumped to Nina, and his wolf gave a baleful cry. Nina was an outsider, too.

He shook his head and turned to Hunter. "You busy tonight?"

Hunter shrugged. Like all bears, the big guy spoke as much with gestures as with words.

"Keep an eye on my place, will you?" Boone said.

Lucky for him it was Hunter and not one of the other guys, all of whom would have launched into an interrogation about why Boone was so concerned for a woman he barely knew.

Because she could be my mate, that's why. The thought shot through his mind. A good thing it didn't slip off his tongue.

Hunter nodded, leaving Boone no choice but to head to Silas's place. Koa Point Estate extended gradually uphill from the private beach where he'd found Nina, past the meeting house, to a craggy cliff a quarter of a mile inland. Earlier, he'd barely noticed the incline, even with Nina in his arms. But now, his steps were heavy and dull. The little stream beside the footpath bubbled as cheerfully as it always did, as if nothing in the world was wrong. The slope steepened, and the path folded into a series of stone steps that carried him toward the cleft in the cliffs. His inner wolf stirred, begging for some climb-and-play time. He loved bounding over those rocks in his free time.

Not now, buddy, he whispered to his inner beast. *Not now.*

Accent lights lay nestled beside the steps, lighting the path as it rose higher toward the estate owner's house. A human might have nicknamed the bold structure *The Eagle's*

Nest or *The Outlook*, but Boone knew what it really was. A dragon's lair. And even though he and the others trusted Silas with their lives, stepping onto Silas's turf always made Boone straighten his shoulders and take a deep breath. The whole place screamed of power and authority even a wolf shifter wouldn't want to mess with. A damn good thing Silas was one of the good guys.

Boone stepped onto the lowest terrace of the sprawling, multistory building and cleared this throat.

A dark, brooding form stood at the end of the terrace, looking out toward the sea. Even with Silas in human form and wearing a tailored suit, it didn't take much imagination to picture a dragon puffing fire then gliding away on huge, leathery wings. That, or spinning and spitting fire at Boone when he heard the news.

"What's this about a woman?" Silas asked without turning. His voice was low and steady. Impossible to read, as always.

Boone shifted his weight from foot to foot. "She washed up on the beach, barely conscious. Says someone tried to kill her by throwing her off a boat."

When Silas turned, the patio light threw his facial features into sharp relief. Even with his bow tie undone, he looked on guard, totally alert. "Someone tried to kill her," he echoed in a flat tone.

Yeah, it did sound crazy. But Boone had seen the fear in Nina's eyes and the bump on her head. "She looked half dead, that's for sure."

Silas studied him so intently, Boone had to remind himself not to squirm.

"Who is she?" Silas asked at last.

Boone bit his lip. *She doesn't remember* sounded pretty lame, but it was true. He'd seen her face go blank as she searched her memories, and he'd seen her eyes well up when she realized she didn't know.

"She only remembers her first name. Nina."

His wolf purred, replaying her name. *Nina. Nina. Nina.*

Silas arched an eyebrow. "She doesn't remember?"

God, he hated it when Silas boomeranged words back at him. He shrugged. "I believe her."

Silas scowled. "She could be making it up."

"Why would she make something like that up?"

"You never know," Silas said with a note of bitterness in his voice.

Boone didn't comment. They'd both been betrayed in the past, but unlike Silas, he didn't hold a grudge against every woman on earth. Still, he kept his mouth shut.

"Where is she now?" Silas asked after a long pause.

"She's asleep."

"Where?" Silas growled.

Boone made damn sure to keep his voice steady as he spoke. "At my place."

Safe and sound, in my bed, his inner wolf hummed.

Silas's thin, arched eyebrows jumped, and he scowled deeply.

Boone bristled and stood his ground. Back when Silas had invited Boone and the others to join his PI/bodyguard crew in Hawaii, they'd agree to a no-humans rule and specified that women were to be entertained elsewhere.

It's not like that, he wanted to assure Silas, but he held his tongue because the words acquired the bitter taste of a lie.

It could be like that, his wolf growled. *I want that.*

Boone clenched his fists so hard that his nails bit into his palms. *It's definitely not like that.*

Silas shook his head. "She can't stay here. No humans. We agreed. You agreed."

That was before I met Nina, Boone wanted to say.

"Whatever trouble she's in, we need to stay clear of," Silas muttered.

Boone figured Silas would say as much. Hiring out to wealthy clients was one thing. Getting personally involved with outsiders was taboo, as it was for all shifters. The less mixing with humans, the better for all concerned. Shifters had to protect the secret of their existence.

"Are you saying I should have kicked her out?" Boone shot back.

Briefly, Silas's expression said, *Why not?* But Silas was a good man at heart — just a little jaded. He made a face and flapped a hand impatiently.

"Bring her to the cops in the morning. Let them handle it."

Warning bells started clanging wildly in Boone's mind, and his wolf reared up.

She's in danger. Can't trust anyone. His wolf shook its head. *Not even the cops.*

It was a hunch he had no rational basis for. Hell, he had no rational explanation for the fierce wave of protective instincts that hammered him every time he thought of Nina.

Why can we protect rich clients but not protect Nina? his wolf went on.

He forced himself to stay calm and count to five. Clients were clients. Easy come, easy go.

We can't let Nina go! his wolf cried.

He shook his head. There was no arguing with his wolf — or with Silas.

"I have to catch an early flight tomorrow, so it's up to you to take care of it," Silas continued.

Boone's wolf hummed. *I'll take care of her, all right.*

But the flight part? His confusion must have showed because Silas drilled him with a hard look. "To Phoenix. Remember?"

Boone covered up quickly. When his mind wasn't obsessed with Nina, yes, he remembered. Silas was heading to Arizona, where he would rendezvous with Kai and Tessa. Kai, a dragon, was the fifth member of their all-shifter group, and Tessa was Kai's mate. Together with Silas, they hoped to track down the treasure stolen years earlier by their archenemy, Damien Morgan, and to investigate Morgan's ties to Drax, a powerful dragon lord. Boone had been itching to accompany the mission himself — until now.

"Maybe Nina will wake up and remember everything," Boone tried.

"Maybe. Either way, let the cops handle it. First thing in the morning."

Silas's words were a final verdict, a gavel slamming on Nina's case — and a dismissal. Boone turned to the stairs, following his cue.

"And Boone?" The note of warning in Silas's voice stopped him short.

He turned around slowly. "Yeah?"

"Remember. We're not getting involved."

He jerked his head into a nod. *Sure. Not getting involved.* But the words sounded hollow, even in his mind.

Chapter Four

At first, Nina slept deep and dreamlessly, well and truly checked out. But then came a restless phase in which nightmares scratched at the edges of her consciousness. Images flashed in her mind — a man's face, bent into a scowl. A long driveway lined with palms. The sight of a tropical shoreline, slipping farther and farther away as her panic grew. Then she was splashing in the sea, desperate to grab hold of something to save herself. An oar smashed down, slicing the water next to her ear.

"No!" she cried, jolting upright and scuttling back in the bed.

It took a minute of hard panting before she realized it had all been a nightmare. She wasn't being attacked for the second time; she was just remembering it.

She sat very still, listening to the sound of the night. Soothing nature sounds like insects chirping, bushes scratching, and waves rolling over a beach. Sounds that told her, *Everything is all right. Go back to sleep.*

Slowly, she settled back onto the pillow. Her shoulder ached, and her ear throbbed. Though her eyes were shut tight, tears leaked out, and she clutched at the fabric under her hand.

"Help," she whispered.

It didn't make sense to call for help, but she couldn't resist the urge. She'd never felt more miserable or more alone.

"Anyone," she croaked, wishing she could be a kid again. Her mom would be in the room next door, and she'd come running any second now.

But there was no one. Nothing but the sound of the sea and her own heaving sobs caused partly by terror, partly by a deep sorrow that had been planted in her soul some time ago. Her mother was dead. Gone. Even without a clear memory of the event, Nina knew.

Get it together, she told herself again and again. But she didn't have it in her just then. Nights were good for crying because nobody else could see. Nights were for hunkering down and getting it all out — the loneliness, the fear, and anxieties — so that the next day, she could dig deep for a smile and the energy to face the world again.

It will be okay, she told herself, stroking her own arm. She could permit herself a little breakdown after nearly being killed, right?

Yes, she could. And whenever daytime came again, she'd be back to her usual self. Positive. Outgoing. Cheerful.

Right now, though... Emotions engulfed her. There was an overwhelming feeling of sadness. A hint of a terrible betrayal. A deep-seated determination not to let life get her down. She sniffed into the pillow, knowing she shouldn't feel sorry for herself.

Happiness is a recipe you create with whatever ingredients life provides. That's what her mom had always said. But damn — that recipe was hard to pin down in the dark.

Curtains danced in the night breeze, and her eyes opened and closed, too weary to look yet too restless to sleep. She caught a glimpse of moonlight glittering over the sea before her eyelids drooped again. That couldn't be real. The scene was too warm, too peaceful. Too *tropical paradise* to be real.

She drifted off again, terrified the nightmare would return. And when footsteps padded up the porch steps, her heart leaped to her throat before she even looked.

A dog stood silhouetted in the doorway, peering in. It whined and wagged its tail.

"Good doggie," Nina whispered, relaxing again.

Dogs were like that, sensing your pain. She'd never had a pet, but her neighbors had a big, furry sheepdog, and she used to bury her face in its fur whenever she felt down. And heck, if she'd had the energy to drag herself out of bed, she would have loved to hug the big dog on the porch. It was fierce yet friendly. A friend, not a foe.

The animal paced across the porch, perking its ears this way and that. Man, it was huge. But that made her feel better, because nothing was getting past that beast. She could see it in the twitch of the dog's nose, the stiff set of its tail. She was safe, and she wasn't alone. Not with that dog there, standing still as a statue. A guard. Her own private sentry.

Her eyelids drooped again, and she let them, leaving the dog — imaginary or real — to chase the last of her nightmares away. She pulled the blanket over her head and curled up on her side.

Everything will be all right. Everything will be okay.

* * *

The next time Nina woke, morning light warmed her back, and a bird sang not too far away. Waves hummed as they rolled upward, then chattered with the drag of pebbles on their way back to the sea. Leaves tickled the windows, and the scent of hibiscus was everywhere.

She had to be dreaming because reality never came close to that kind of peace. Reality was alarm clocks and crushing debt and crowded streets. Reality was the ache that came from losing someone you loved and the weariness you felt after too many hours on your feet. The loneliness of waking up alone, day after day.

The trick to life is making the best of what you have. Even millionaires have problems, you know.

Nina smiled into the sheets as her mother's voice echoed through her mind. Her mother was right, of course. There was beauty in everyday things, like sharing a smile, even if it was with a stranger. There was beauty in waking up to another day and going about your routine.

Nina kept her eyes closed, determined to drift around in her dream as long as she could. But even as her senses woke one by one, the dreamy feeling persisted. The coconut oil and salt-air scent still tickled her nose. The ocean continued to murmur not far from where she lay. The balmy air soothed her skin, and light stroked her back, making her feel like a cat curled up on a windowsill for a snooze.

She cracked one eye open, then another, and blinked a few times, afraid of what would happen if she moved. Would the throbbing in her head return? Would the nausea? Slowly, she focused on the bedside table. No clock there — just a conch shell bigger than her foot. She looked around. Where was she?

Curtains flapped lazily in the wide-open windows and doorways, the light fabric swaying with a sea breeze. Colored bottles stood along the crossbeams of the cottage's rustic walls, reflecting the light in tiny beams of green, brown, and red. There were rocks, too, and more shells — all in all, a beachcomber's treasure trove. The calendar tacked to one wall was ragged at the edges and — she squinted — two years old. Whoever lived in the cottage probably kept it for the detailed map printed in the center rather than to keep track of time. The whole bungalow was like that — a bright, sunny place that beat away all sense of time. She had no idea how long she'd slept or how she'd arrived there.

Then the gears in her mind lurched into action, and it all came back. The handsome stranger who'd held her tight. The deep, gentle voice that had wished her goodnight. The strong arms that had made her feel impossibly safe after the nightmare she'd endured.

She jolted upright, clutching the sheets. "Oh God."

Someone had tried to kill her out on the ocean. She touched her head and found the lump. She'd managed to swim to shore, where she might have drowned in the shallows if her knight in shining armor hadn't come along.

Boone. That was his name. She remembered that clearly. He was Boone, and she was. . .

She clutched the sheets tighter, because other than *Nina*, her mind was blank.

She hunched over her knees and hugged herself, rocking quietly. All sense of peace had fled, replaced by a feeling of dread. Images of home — her real home — passed through her mind in a blurry rush, and it was nothing like this. It was cold, for one thing. Wintery cold, with snow to be shoveled and ice to be negotiated on the long walk to the bus stop that would bring her to work.

Work. Oh God. She had to be incredibly late, though she couldn't remember where she worked or what her job was, except that the thought came with the image of a big, jolly man and the jingle of a bell over a door. Wherever home was, it had to be miles away.

She stood quickly, ignoring the aches that flared all over her body, and went to the map on the wall. A predominantly green map with a fringe of blue and a two-lobed island labeled in happy, cartoon letters. *Maui.*

She peeked outside and saw the silvery-blue sea framed by palms. How on earth did she get to Maui? Despite the huge blanks in her mind, she was sure of one thing. People like her didn't go to Hawaii, because Hawaii was really far and really expensive. She might as well be in a casino in Monte Carlo or an exclusive resort in Bali.

But, holy cow. She really was in Hawaii. That, or her mind was completely messed up.

She steadied herself against the open framing of the walls, then took a piece of red sea glass and held it up to the sun, figuring it was better to focus on something small. Color poured through it, making her think of life. Of blood. Of fire. That glass was red like a ruby, and though red was the color of danger, the effect soothed her soul.

"How are you doing?"

She had every right to shriek at the voice that came out of nowhere, but she didn't. That voice made her feel safe. Protected. Cherished, even. Which only went to prove how bad that knock on her head had been.

She turned and nodded to Boone, who was standing in the doorway.

The last hour of sleep had been filled with images of a too-good-to-be-true man, and yet there he was, in the flesh. His eyes were as blue as the sky. His smile was genuine, his voice filled with concern just as it had been the previous night when he'd carried her.

Her blood rushed. Her heart thumped, and her voice caught in her throat.

"Um. . . I'm good," she squeaked while her mind raced.

He cocked his head. "Good, as in you're just saying you feel good, or actually good?"

She laughed. Yes, there'd been plenty of times in her life when she'd fibbed the answer to that question — even with the blanks in her mind, she knew that — but right now, she meant it.

"Actually good," she murmured, suddenly aware of how little she was wearing and how closely she'd been snuggled against his chest the previous night.

Goose bumps broke out over her arms, and she rubbed herself. Her skin itched. Her bikini was stiff and salty, which was handy in hiding the way her nipples peaked in reaction to him. Her hair was plastered to her scalp like dried seaweed.

"Well, I could use a shower."

"A shower," he echoed, looking at her. "You're amazing. After all you've been through. . . "

She stared. She wasn't amazing. She was just plain old her.

The way he shook his head told her she was anything but plain, and they stood gazing at each other for a good minute, suddenly stuck in time. The sound of the waves grew faint, as did the rustle of leaves, and Nina couldn't help leaning forward. Electricity zapped in the air, and invisible waves of heat bounced between her body and his. Was the man a magician? Could he weave a spell and draw her in at will?

But Boone was leaning in, too, and as dreamy-eyed as she. So whatever the magic was, it worked on them both, swirling around, creating a little bubble of warmth and peace and positive energy. Her heart rate slowed, and a yearning for something she didn't know she was missing put a lump in her throat.

Then a sea gull cried overhead, and *poof!* The bubble burst.

"Oh!" Nina exclaimed as the events of the previous night clicked back into her mind. "You saved me."

He shook his head. "You saved yourself. All I did was dry you off."

Nina gulped. There wasn't a hint of sauciness in his comment, and yet her pulse raced at the idea.

He ran a hand through his rumpled hair, and suddenly, she was mortified. "Did you give me your bed? I'm so sorry. Where did you sleep last night?"

He looked out the front door and sniffed the breeze at exactly the angle the dog in her dream had.

"I was fine. Don't worry. Did you sleep okay?"

She nodded in quick, jerky movements, figuring that was better than the truth. *Yes and no. I had the weirdest dreams. First, someone was trying to drown me again, and then a huge dog stood guard over me.*

"Do you have a dog?" she asked, peeking outside. The dog had seemed so real...

"No dog." His lips twitched and she was sure he would add something, but he didn't. Eventually, he cleared his throat and changed the subject. "I was thinking you could use some lunch..."

Nina opened her mouth. Lunch? Had she really slept that long?

Boone motioned over his shoulder. "But you'd probably like that shower first."

A shower would be heaven — or as close to heaven as she'd just been in that bubble of her and him.

"A shower would be nice," she said, looking around.

The little bungalow was one big, open space with a tiny bathroom, no kitchen, and no shower. Boone motioned through the double front doors. They were wide open, making the inside of the cottage seem as fresh and airy as the beach. She stepped onto the porch that wrapped around the front, surveying her surroundings from the top of four steps. A striped hammock hung on the porch, along with an antique glass fishing float. A flagstone walkway led to the beach, just a few steps away. A bamboo rack to the left held a couple of surfboards and a sun-bleached towel.

"The shower is right there. I brought you a fresh towel," he murmured, suddenly very much a little boy.

She took it, wondering if that was a blush on his cheeks. God, he was cute — cute as in *your-body-belongs-on-a-poster* cute, and cute as in puppy-dog cute, though she couldn't explain exactly how those two combined.

She followed his gesture. To the right side of the house stood a stone wall shaded by lush plants with big, waxy leaves. Something silver glinted, and she stepped closer. Was that really...? Wow. It really was a shower. A gorgeous outdoor shower that promised half her worries would be solved just by stepping in.

Boone mumbled something about privacy and hurried over to the beach, keeping his back turned. Nina stared for a second, biting her lip. The man was essentially a stranger. Was she really going to trust him not to turn around?

He stood facing the sea, and the hard set of his shoulders was the same as his face the night before: all promise, all protection. No fooling around.

Nina bit her lip, looking at him. Well, the shower was half hidden by foliage. And if she showered fast...

Flicking the water on and testing it with one hand, she found it warm and soft — much softer than the salt water crusted on her skin. She tugged the knot on her bikini, slipped off the bottom half, and stepped in. The shower head was huge, making the stream of water so broad, it felt like standing under a waterfall in an island paradise. And wow, did it feel good — even better than sleeping in Boone's huge, homey bed. The light touch of her hands on her body was comforting, too, though the dirty part of her mind had all kinds of bad ideas, like inviting Boone over to do her back. Her front, too.

He could do me all over, her inner vixen said.

In the distance, Boone kicked at the sand and cleared his throat. Nina chastised herself, splashing water as she tried to trade dirty thoughts for more innocent subjects, like how lucky she was to be alive. Boone hadn't said a thing, but the bump on her head was all the reminder she needed that someone had tried to kill her the previous night.

Bit by bit, the soap cleansed more than just her skin, and the vanilla-scented shampoo felt like liquid silk in her hair.

By the time she forced herself out of the shower and wrapped herself in the fluffy towel, she felt human again. Ready to face whatever harsh trials life threw her way.

"You all set?" Boone called, still facing the beach.

"Yes."

He turned and ambled up. "Perfect. I'll just get you..."

His words slowed as he came closer, and his eyes locked on hers. And there it was again — the magic bubble closing in, cocooning them away from the world. His eyes glowed indigo, and though Nina knew it had to be a trick of the light, she was mesmerized. Those eyes were so deep, so honest. So desperate for something.

A drop of water slid from her hair to her chest, gliding slowly between her breasts. The heat pooled in her body, and every breath felt deeper, slower. Heavier, like a great truth was about to be revealed. A great dam of words built in her mind, though none of them made sense and she didn't utter a sound.

"Boone?" a voice boomed from the distance, and they both snapped around. "You coming?"

Boone gave himself a little shake before calling back. "Be right there."

Nina pulled the towel higher — right up to her chin, hiding behind it like a shy schoolgirl. A good thing, too, because it felt like she'd been seconds away from dropping the towel and inviting Boone into her embrace. God, what was wrong with her? And what was up with him? Boone was all laid-back and easygoing on the outside, but underneath, the man was pure intensity. All raw, animal power that called to her, body and soul.

"I'll get you a shirt," he mumbled, brushing past her, up the three stairs.

She dried quickly and slipped her bikini back on. It was all she had, and suddenly, she felt lower and lonelier than she'd ever felt before. Then Boone bounded out of the bungalow, filled with a new burst of puppy-dog energy, and held up a blue T-shirt and the Hawaiian print sarong that had been draped over the couch inside.

"What do you think?" The animal side of him had disappeared, and now he was all surfer dude with a huge grin and and mischievous eyes. "I think you'll be more comfortable in these than in the other stuff I have. Unless you like camo shorts." He winked, sticking a thumb in the pocket of the cargo cutoffs he wore.

"I think these are more my style," she said, wrapping the sarong over her bikini bottom, then pulling on the T-shirt. It was three sizes too big, so she twirled a corner and tied a knot at one side.

"I think so, too," he murmured as his eyes bounced away, then back to her, then away again, as if he really did like what he saw. And when she finger-combed her hair, he nodded as if looking at a princess or fashion queen instead of a castaway.

"Lunch time. You hungry?" he murmured, ever so softly.

Starving, her inner voice purred.

She moved her lips a few times, struggling to answer. "A little," she said, managing to sound casual despite the heat building in her cheeks.

Boone grinned, and when she gazed into his bright blue eyes, she felt lost — and found — all over again.

Chapter Five

Nina followed as Boone led her up a winding path, past patches of neatly trimmed lawn that alternated with dense knots of vegetation. She was barefoot, and it felt nice to stride over the lush, springy grass. A stream gurgled somewhere in the distance, and a yellow butterfly fluttered over bright red flowers.

"Hibiscus," Boone murmured, and for some reason, she blushed.

All the colors, the scents, the sounds piqued her senses, and the energy that had drained out of her the night before came trickling back in. Boone was part of that, too, making her mind come alive, bringing the smile back to her face.

She spotted a rooftop poking up behind a tall hedge — another dwelling on what seemed to be a sizable estate — and a square of cement with a big H painted in the middle. A helipad?

"You live here?" She gaped, looking around. Well, of course, he lived there. But the estate seemed too big and manicured for a man like Boone. The rustic beach bungalow suited him to a T, but the rest of the place didn't seem to fit.

Boone laughed. "What? Don't I seem like a millionaire playboy with my own seaside estate?"

"No," she said without thinking then backpedaled wildly. "I mean, it's not that... um..."

He grinned a mile wide. "Don't worry. I'll take that as a compliment."

Nina found herself grinning, too, but then they turned a corner and emerged at a big, open-walled building set in the middle of a closely clipped lawn. She stopped in her tracks, mumbling. "I remember this..."

Boone nodded eagerly. "That's good. You were here last night. Do you remember further back than that?"

She closed her eyes, willing that to be the case. But the only information her mind surrendered was frantic images of swimming for her life and memories from much further back, like sitting cuddled with her mother on a worn but cozy couch, reading *Frog and Toad Are Friends.* A bittersweet smile drifted over her lips.

"Nothing?" Boone coaxed her along.

"Nothing." She shook her head a little. Why couldn't she remember anything?

"That's okay," he murmured, making her feel less like a hopeless case. "It will be all right. A little lunch goes a long way, right?" He motioned ahead. "That's our *akule hale* — the meeting house."

She followed him toward the building, wishing she didn't have to face anyone else right now. Walking barefoot beside Boone was easy and comfortable, but the thought of anyone else made her worry about her hair, her face, and — oh God — the pathetic impression she must have made the previous night.

"Will the others be there?"

Boone must have heard the anxiety in her voice because he gave her shoulder a reassuring squeeze. "Don't worry. Silas left early this morning, and the other guys... Well, they're all bark and no bite. Hiya, Hunter," he called, stepping into the shade of the building.

A big, burly guy with brown hair and a neatly trimmed beard stood quickly — old-fashioned manners, Nina thought, warming inside — and nodded.

"How do you do?" he asked, ever so politely. Shyly, almost.

"I feel a lot better, thank you," she said, turning to the second man as Boone made for the coffeepot.

Hunter put her immediately at ease, but the second man — not as big but lithe and corded with muscle — scowled. Cruz — that was his name. His striking yellow-green eyes pierced hers as he grumbled under his breath. "Does she remember anything?"

He said it as if she weren't even there. As if she were a piece of flotsam that had washed up on the beach.

Nina looked at the floor. Well, it wasn't that far from the truth. And Cruz was probably just cranky from her interrupting their evening, so it was her fault, not his.

But Boone didn't seem as quick to forgive. He stalked over to the dark-haired man with a murderous look on his face. "Hunter, show Nina what we have while I talk to Cruz."

Nina bit her lip. Boone's expression sure didn't look like *talking* was what he had in mind. Cruz looked as dark and dangerous as Boone had suddenly become, and she worried there would be a fight.

Hunter moved past her, faster than a man that size ought to have been able to move, and thrust himself between the two men who stood bristling and growling at each other like a couple of wild beasts.

"Sure," Hunter said, in a voice that was both soft and powerful. "You two talk. Talk." He emphasized the last word and shoved the two of them out into the noon sun.

Nina stood, chewing her lip, but Hunter just sighed. "Don't worry about them. Come and eat."

Reluctantly, with a last glance over her shoulder, she followed Hunter to the kitchen section of the expansive living space. There was a living room area with several couches, a dining area with a table big enough for ten, and a reading nook she longed to curl up in.

"Help yourself," Hunter said, motioning toward the refrigerator while he drew a plate out of a cabinet for her.

The place seemed like one big bachelor pad, and Nina braced herself for what she might find inside the fridge. Jars of pickles and cans of beer? But the shelves were full of neatly arranged packages and fresh produce — so much, she hardly knew where to start.

Her surprise must have shown because Hunter chuckled. "Tessa made us promise to eat well while she was away."

"Who's Tessa?" Nina asked quickly, suddenly eager for female company.

"She's Kai's ma—" He stalled out on one word and finished with another. "Kai's partner. A chef. They're, um... honeymooning for a couple of weeks."

She'd never thought about it before, but heck, if she lived in Hawaii, she could honeymoon at home.

Honeymoon... A dark memory raced in and out of her mind, too quickly to catch.

"Would you like me to make you a sandwich, too?" she asked, resisting the chill that swept over her mind.

Hunter nodded eagerly.

"Let me guess. Ham and cheese with mustard and a little honey," she tried.

His jaw dropped.

"I have a knack for guessing." The grin that came as easily as the words turned into a frown when she realized what she'd just said. How did she know what she had a knack for? Did it have to do with a hobby or what she did for a living?

"Hey," Boone murmured, coming up behind her. "Did you find something you like?"

The sound of his voice halted the sinking feeling in her gut, pushing the *what's wrong with me* worries away.

She nodded, not trusting her voice yet, and started pulling out cold cuts, condiments, and lettuce. She tried guessing what Boone would like. "Roast beef for you?"

He nodded, helping her set up. Cruz, she noticed, kept his distance, eyeing her from the perimeter of the space like a lion from a cage. There was something decidedly feline about the way he paced — all power, all masculine, all pent-up frustration. She looked away quickly. Why did she have the feeling every man here had a hidden, feral side? That and a past filled with pain and regret, for all that each covered it up. Even quiet Hunter, the biggest and quietest of the group, carried a hint of sadness about him.

She slabbed mustard on the bread Boone handed her in heavy strokes and added several slices of salami.

"What happened to roast beef?" he asked, raising an eyebrow.

She pointed to the second sandwich — the one with extra tomato. "That's yours. That one is for Hunter, and this one is for him. Cruz, right?" She called his name cheerily. Whatever had happened between Cruz and Boone was her fault, and she wanted to extend a peace offering. "Do you like salami?"

Cruz glowered at her from the shadows, then gave a curt nod.

"Perfect," she murmured brightly, pretending he'd lavished her with praise. Some guys were just cranky, and little gestures went a long way, even if the man didn't let on right away. How she knew that, she wasn't sure. But somehow, she knew it was true.

She, Boone, and the others all clustered around the bar that extended from the kitchen — even Cruz, who perched on a barstool at the far end — and chowed down on their lunches. Nina relished every bite of her turkey sandwich and soaked in the happy sound of munching all around. She'd been famished, and the men looked like it, too.

"You guys eat like a pack of wolves," she joked.

Boone choked on his sandwich, and Hunter thumped his back, flashing her a huge grin. "You could say that."

"Great sandwich," Boone said, covering up whatever had thrown him.

Even Cruz appeared to hide a little chuckle, and she wondered what she'd just said. Whatever it was, the tension in the room continued to ease, and that felt good. She stood for the coffeepot and made a round of everyone's mug.

"Refill?" she asked Hunter.

"Sure. Thanks."

She pushed the sugar and cream his way. "Pass the cream to Boone when you're done."

"Whoa," Boone murmured, putting his hand over his mug.

"No more for you?"

"I do want more, but how did you know I take milk and no sugar?"

She shrugged, making her shoulder ache. "I saw you make it before. Hunter takes both, you take milk, and Cruz drinks his black. Right?"

They all stared at her for a second before Boone cracked into a smile. "I've been living with these morons for years, and they still don't remember how I take my coffee."

"As if you remember how I take mine," Hunter sighed.

They chuckled, though Nina winced a little at the word *remember*. "I guess you just have to pay attention to the little things."

Boone saved her plummeting mood with a broad smile and a wink. "Come to think of it, I can't even remember these guys' birthdays."

Nina smiled and sat quietly, hoping her own birthday might pop into her mind. But three different dates floated around in that foggy haze, and none felt exactly right. But at least there was that — the blank area was slowly filling with blurry shapes, sounds, and emotions. Maybe if she gave herself a few more days, her memory would return.

She looked around. Did she even have a couple of days? Would they let her stay? Wouldn't her family miss her while she was gone?

She downed the last of her sandwich with a long gulp of coffee, trying to swallow the vague sense that she didn't have anyone who might miss her.

"So, what next?" she murmured, looking at Boone.

He grinned. "Next? Cruz does the dishes—"

Cruz muttered something under his breath, but Boone just laughed.

"—and you and I go to town to investigate what's going on."

"Whoa," Hunter said. "Silas didn't say investigate. He said to go to the police."

Boone stood, tugging Nina's hand gently. "Someone tried to kill her. Someone who probably thinks she's dead. And dead is safer than alive, don't you think?"

Nina didn't know what to think — only that an icy chill crept down her spine. Someone did try to kill her. Had she done something awful to deserve it or was it all a terrible mistake?

Hunter seemed dubious, but Boone just tugged her along. "We will go to the police — eventually. But it won't hurt to look around first. Right?"

The first part of Boone's question was aimed at Hunter, but the second was aimed squarely at Nina, and she managed a nod. "Right."

"Hang on. Where are you going to start?" Hunter said. "You need a plan."

"Such a bea—" Boone started, then coughed.

Bear? Nina chuckled. Hunter definitely was a bear of a man.

Hunter shot Boone a look of warning, but the smile he gave Nina was genuine. Caring. "What do you remember?"

Nina bit her lip. The man was sweet, putting it that way instead of emphasizing what she *couldn't* remember. Which was a lot. She stammered and did her best to reply, but her mind kept serving up blanks, and her tongue kept getting stuck on how exactly to put the blur into words.

"Can you ID the men who pushed you off the boat?" Boone asked.

She closed her eyes and caught a brief flash of a strangely familiar face. One moment it was there, sneering in her memory, and the next, the face of her would-be killer was gone.

She shook her head. "No. I don't think I can."

"What about the boat? Was it a runabout? A cruiser? A sport fishing boat?"

The men looked at her expectantly, but heck. She couldn't tell one end of a boat from the other. How could she describe a boat she only remembered in snippets?

"It's okay," Boone murmured. "I'm sure you'll remember when you have something to spark your memory. We'll start at the marina."

Hunter didn't look convinced, but Boone was so sure of himself — no, sure of her — that it gave her confidence, too.

"Sure," she murmured, though her knees threatened to lock up.

"We won't be long," Boone told the others as he stood and took her hand.

He led her away from the building and up a long, winding driveway to what looked like a stable, although it turned out to be a garage full of exotic cars. Nina's eyes went wide as Boone led her past a Ferrari, a vintage Jaguar, a Land Rover, and a Mercedes S class, all waxed and polished until they shone brighter than the sun. Who owned this place? And which was Boone's car? She pictured him in a beat-up pickup with a surfboard on the roof, but when he turned left into the last archway of the long, sprawling building, she spotted a motorcycle. A big, black Harley.

She hung back a little, suddenly unsure. "What if they see me?"

They were the men who'd tried to kill her, and Boone seemed to understand, because he took her shaking hand. "No one will be able to see you." He held up a helmet with a tinted visor. "See?"

She nodded but didn't budge one inch.

"No one will see you, Nina. But I'm hoping you'll see something that sparks a memory."

She gulped. "What if I don't? What, then?"

He curled his lips inward, holding back whatever answer had nearly rolled off his tongue. "If you prefer to go straight to the cops, I can take you. I'll take you anywhere you want to go."

She had no idea where she wanted to go. Only that she wanted to stay close to him. Not so much from the fear of who was out there as from the overwhelming feeling that she belonged with him. As if destiny was watching at exactly that moment and signaling her wildly from behind Boone's back. *This guy. Believe me, you want to stick with this guy.*

She gulped. Why was it that nothing was clear to her except that?

Boone waited quietly, hope shining in his eyes.

"No cops," she murmured. "Not yet."

He broke into a smile so wide, so sunny, that she grinned, too.

"We'll look around town then figure out what to do next. I promise I'll take care of you," he murmured, going all warrior on her again.

She'd never been the need-to-be-taken-care-of type, but at that very moment, his words gave her the shot of confidence she needed. So much that she rolled onto her toes and kissed him on the cheek. No more than a quick, chaste peck, really, but still, her heart leaped.

Boone blinked, standing perfectly still except for the vein pulsing in his neck.

"Thanks," she whispered.

"For what?" His voice was hushed.

"For helping me. For everything."

He bit his lip, and his eyes seemed to glow. Her heart beat faster, because they were slipping into that bubble again. Then he gave himself a little shake and nodded. "For you, Nina — anything."

He kissed her knuckles and kept them pressed to his lips as his eyes closed. Nina closed hers, too, savoring that feeling of connection, of trust. She'd been so alone for so long — that much was perfectly clear in her mind, even if the circumstances were not — and somehow, this perfect stranger felt like a lifetime friend.

"Ready?" he whispered.

She nodded. Boone helped her slide the helmet on. His touch was tender and careful, and when she had it on, he smoothed her hair back from her cheek and tucked it carefully inside.

"All set," he said, though his voice was muffled now that she had the helmet on. He slid her visor down, and a gray layer covered her field of vision. That made her feel safe, too.

Boone pulled on another helmet, walked the bike out of the garage, and straddled it. When he nodded her onto the back, she went without hesitation and snuggled up behind him like they'd gone riding together dozens of times.

"All set," she murmured, hanging on to his waist.

Chapter Six

The moment Nina slid into place behind him, Boone's inner wolf howled. A good howl — the way he used to do when the moon was high and life was simple and good. So good, he had to celebrate with a long, wolf cry of joy — like the one he'd forced himself to hold back last night when he'd peeked in and seen Nina in his bed.

Damn. When was the last time he'd wanted to howl for the sheer joy of it? Ages. A decade, maybe, way back when before he'd enlisted. Before he'd left the Southwest. Before Tammy had stomped all over his heart.

"Everything okay?" Nina asked in a soft, silky voice when he didn't make a move to start the bike. He was too busy digesting that feeling and what it might mean.

"Great," he murmured, kicking the engine to life. Then he settled back on the seat and took off, telling himself it was just like any other ride on any other day.

Sure, his wolf said. *Right. Just a regular old ride with my mate. Happens every day.*

He took a deep breath, which only tightened Nina's hold around his waist. And man, did that feel nice. As nice as seeing her smile at him that morning had been.

It turned out to be a ride of many firsts, actually, starting with the fact that he didn't get pulled over by Officer Meli, the female cop who always staked out this stretch of the Honoapi'ilani Highway and caught him for something every time. It was almost a game between the two of them, but he didn't have time for games today. Not with Nina to keep out of the public eye. So he made damn sure to keep five miles under the speed limit and drive in a nice, straight line instead of slaloming in and out of the median. The funny thing was, driving according to the rules didn't even feel like torture for a change. Maybe because Nina was there, giving him all the joy he needed.

He looked left at the second turn and, yep — there was Officer Meli, already easing her cruiser forward in anticipation. But then she hit the brakes with a look of surprise on her face. Boone grinned.

No ticket today. That was different, for sure. The ride was different, too. How was it that he'd never noticed the deep blue of the sea or the rich fragrance of the coffee plantation upslope of the road? It was the first time he paid attention to the potholes, too, because Nina had been through enough, and her grip around his waist was still a little unsure. The less he rattled her around, the better.

You're right. She doesn't like being rattled, his wolf agreed as if he already knew everything about Nina.

Boone scoffed, but his wolf insisted. *We know the important things.*

He had to give the wolf that much. He might not know a lot about Nina, but maybe he really did know the important things. She was genuine. She took care of others before taking care of herself, like she had at lunch. She wasn't rich, but she wasn't judgmental, either. And she certainly wasn't the type to go for joyrides on the back of some guy's bike.

He grimaced. Nina didn't even know she was riding with a wolf shifter, and that was the one thing that marred his good mood. He felt like a liar, hiding the truth about who he was. But he could hardly come out and say, *Nina, there's something you need to know about me.* Where would he start?

Not only am I a wolf shifter, but I'm a total wash-up who hasn't been able to get his shit together in the past few years. Hunter says I'm avoiding coping with the past, and I have the sinking feeling he's right.

"Wow," Nina cried, pointing to the right.

He pulled over to let her ooh and ahh at a whale breeching in the distance. Nina deserved that little bit of joy and wonder after all she'd been through.

"There's a baby, too!" she cried.

That set his wolf into fantasies of a whole new kind.

Pups. With Nina. Would be nice, huh?

Boone scuffed the earth with his shoe and counted to ten.

"Ready to go?" he asked once the whales had stopped the show.

Nina sighed — a deep, happy sigh, as if the whales had given her a reason to remember how good life could be. And there was another thing he knew about her — Nina believed in good. In the joy of life. He could see it in her smile and her hopeful gaze.

"Ready," she said.

Boone drove on, trying to ignore the emotions roiling in his gut. He was supposed to help Nina find out who she was and what had happened, not to be thinking about *forever* with a woman like her.

A sign for the police station flashed by, but Boone didn't slow down one bit. Silas wanted him to wash his hands of Nina's case, but there was no way he would treat Nina like a lost dog you dropped off at the animal shelter, hoping the poor thing would do okay. His gut insisted no one could help her — and more importantly, protect her — as well as he could.

"You okay?" he shouted over his shoulder when her hands tightened hard enough to push the breath out of him.

"Um...yes," she mumbled, though her whole body was stiff.

Had she just remembered something? Boone looked around for what might have set her off. A truck loaded with pineapples had just passed going the other way, leaving a sweet scent in its wake. They'd just driven by the gates to the exclusive Kapa'akea Resort on the ocean side of the road, but he doubted that had set her off. Nina wasn't the ritzy, pretentious kind. So maybe it was the truck?

"Are you sure?"

She nodded against his back, so he didn't push it.

Traffic slowed as they entered the town limits of Lahaina, and he could sense Nina swiveling her head from side to side, taking in the historic town. Despite the touristy feel, it was a pretty place, full of funky shops and century-old buildings painted in crisp white and brilliant blues or greens. He went at a snail's pace, letting her enjoy it, knowing there would be harder things to face soon. Very soon.

Like when he pulled over and halted the bike at the edge of the marina. Nina had said she'd been cast into the sea from a boat, so. . .

"Do you recognize anything?" he asked, killing the engine but keeping his helmet on.

The Harley was perfectly still, but Nina clutched at his ribs. When she spoke, her voice was jittery.

"A boat like that." She clamped down on his arm and looked at a sport fishing boat that was gliding out of the harbor. "Mostly white. But the name was written in gold on the back. Something with an A. Angel's. . . Angel's something."

He patted her hand, wishing he could do something to make her feel at ease. "Good. You're remembering."

"I'm not sure I want to remember."

Boone knew the feeling. Some experiences were so bad, you didn't want to revisit them, not even in your mind. But if he didn't track down who was after Nina and why, she wouldn't be safe.

"Hey," he said, turning to her. They were so close, their helmets bumped. So close, his body warmed with need. "One step at a time, right?"

Her eyes were as big and watery as a puppy's, and his heart ached, seeing her like that.

"One thing at a time," she echoed quietly.

He would have liked to walk the docks with Nina and check out one boat at a time, but he could hardly parade a near-murder victim around in public. Nina might see her attackers, but then again, they might spot her first.

"No problem." He started the bike up again. "We'll look up every boat registered on Maui with *Angel* in the name and take it from there."

"You can do that?"

He patted his wallet. "Private investigator's license doesn't hurt."

Like all the other guys at Koa Point, he had his P.I. license. They'd joked about it at first, calling each other *Dragon, P.I.* and *Werewolf, P.I.* like so many characters from a TV show. But the license had come in handy for some of the jobs he took on from time to time.

Nina gawked at him, and he couldn't help but wonder what her line of work was. Something with people, for sure. Something that made good use of the smile that came so readily to her — when she wasn't struggling to remember who'd tried to kill her, that was. Was she a teacher? A doctor? Maybe a physiotherapist? But why would anyone want to kill a person like her? Nina was so normal. So nice. So kind.

When he took off again, she pressed up against his back, setting off a dozen heated fantasies. If only things were different, he could be taking her on a joyride, and she might even sneak her hands lower, giving him a subtle signal of what she wanted. He'd rev the engine to coax a laugh out of her and eventually pull over at an overlook. They'd look out at the sea together, then turn and gaze into each other's eyes. He dreamed of Nina pulling her helmet off and shaking that beautiful hair out again. Then, from one heartbeat to another, she'd go all serious, and her gaze would drop to his lips.

Kiss me, her body would sing, calling to his.

And dang, his body was already singing back, wishing it weren't just a fantasy.

But maybe it wasn't, because Nina's hands really did dip a fraction lower, and her breasts pressed into his back. He could swear her heart started beating faster, and not just from the ride. Maybe he could take her to a secret waterfall where the two of them could—

A passing car tooted at another, pulling Boone's mind back to reality.

Research. We're doing research, he told himself. *Nothing else.*

His wolf grumbled. *Right. Sure. Nothing else.*

He cruised as far as Maalaea and even made a detour up into the West Maui mountains, hoping for Nina to point and cry out, *That's it! I remember everything now!* Or better yet, for her to motion him to the side of the road and play out the scene he'd imagined all too clearly. But she remained perfectly still and quiet — until he headed back up the coast to Koa Point, when she squeezed his waist and sucked in a sharp breath.

He glanced over his shoulder at her, but she was looking back. "What?"

She tilted her head. "I'm not sure."

Boone checked the side mirror and looped back over the same section of road, slowing down when her fingers squeezed his ribs.

"I know that place," she said over the noise of the engine.

He slowed down, looking right. "You sure?"

It was hard to keep the skepticism out of his voice, because that was the Kapa'akea Resort, one of the most exclusive resorts on Maui. Maybe *the* most exclusive resort. A place where the rich and famous played golf, celebrated weddings, and threw extravagant parties. He'd been there once on a bodyguarding job, and hell, he'd never seen so many haughty people in his life. Totally not Nina's scene, unless she'd worked for the catering crew.

A long row of swaying palms lined the driveway, and a curve at the end kept the buildings out of sight. All he could see were a couple of impeccably trimmed golf links and a red-roofed guard house.

"I know it," Nina insisted, gripping his shoulders tightly. Her voice had more fear than anticipation in it.

He made another U-turn and slowly cruised down the driveway to the resort. A guy like him had a snowball's chance in hell of making it past the security checkpoint, but heck. Maybe getting closer would help Nina remember something — or to come to the conclusion that she was wrong about the place.

A rotund security officer stepped out of the guard house, hitched up his pants, and put up a hand in a stop sign. He didn't bother smiling, and Boone could read the disdain all over the guy's face.

Should have taken the Ferrari, his wolf grumbled.

"Can I help you?" the guard demanded as a second man came out. A tall guy. Backup, Boone figured, ready to assist his partner if their unexpected guests so much as lifted a finger. What did they think he was going to do, bust right through the gate with his bike?

Nina leaned out and took off her helmet for a closer look at the place. When her silky hair cascaded over his shoulder, his mind went blank. Blissfully, blindly blank. Her vanilla-honeysuckle scent swept over him, and he just about sighed instead of composing a cover story to explain to the security guard why he and Nina were there.

An explanation they didn't need, as it turned out, because the guard's stern look faded the second he spotted Nina.

"Oh! It's you, miss."

Boone and Nina both did a double take.

"Good to see you again, miss," the tall one stammered, stepping back.

The heavyset guy went from arrogant to sniveling in the blink of an eye. "So sorry, miss. We didn't know it was you."

Boone peeked over his shoulder at Nina, who looked about as shocked as he was. They knew Nina? How?

One guard stepped to the side while the other hurried to lift the barrier, and they both stood at attention, waiting for Boone to pass.

He wanted to gape at Nina and ask, *Are you a princess or something?* But this was his chance, and he took it, cruising down the drive before the guards had second thoughts.

"What was that about?" he called over his shoulder as he drove on.

"I have no idea," Nina said, sounding more rattled than ever.

He took the curve slowly, trying to think. A dozen polo ponies thundered by the field beside the road, making the earth rumble as their riders brandished sticks, chasing the ball. Instinctively, Boone threw an arm around Nina, as if that were the danger, when in fact the danger was the unknown.

Then the resort came into view — a sprawling, six-story, hacienda style building. A valet stepped forward, wavering at the sight of the motorcycle. Boone cruised right past him and parked at the end of the lot.

"What do we do now?" Nina asked, blinking rapidly.

Funny, he wanted to ask her that.

"Do you really remember this place?"

She gulped and nodded. "I know it. Don't ask me how, but I know it. That valet's name is Toby, and the two guys at the gate were Mr. Pilger and Mr. Lee."

She knew the staff's names? Boone nodded slowly. Maybe Nina really did have a catering job. But that wouldn't account for the guards treating her like a movie star, so he was still stumped.

"Okay," he said, drawing the word out. "I guess we have two choices."

Her brow folded into worried lines.

"One, we walk in there like we own the place and hope they don't call our bluff."

Nina's eyes went wide in alarm. "Or?"

"Or we get the hell out of here and do some investigating from home."

That was the chickenshit option, and Boone knew it, but highfalutin places like this didn't agree with him one bit. The last time he'd been here, the fabulously wealthy thirtysomething widow of an oil tycoon had tried to coax him into her bed. When he refused, she'd made a face and pulled out a stack of hundred-dollar bills as if he were a stallion for hire who would put out simply because someone told him to.

No thanks.

Nina nodded — quickly, as if keeping her nerve up. "Let's go in."

She slid off the bike before he could say a word and ran her fingers through her long, shiny hair. Hair he longed to touch. To stroke. To turn in his fist and tug her in for a kiss.

Mate, his wolf hummed. *She is my mate.*

He gulped as Nina adjusted her windblown sarong. His heart thumped faster, saying the same thing.

Mate. My destined mate.

He cleared his throat and dismounted, trying to keep his mind on the business at hand. It was risky, letting Nina be seen, but she was right. They'd make more progress by tracking down whatever was familiar about this place than by avoiding it.

She hooked her helmet on the handlebar and took his hand. A moment later, she looked down as if just realizing what she'd done and murmured, "I hope you don't mind."

He wound his fingers through hers. A perfect fit.

"Nah. I don't mind," he said, trying to play it cool. Almost succeeding, until he slipped up and confessed, "It's kind of nice."

A monumental understatement, because every nerve in his body sang with joy at her touch.

She smiled, and his blood all rushed south. "It is nice."

Hand in hand, they walked to the entrance as if they were a couple of happy honeymooners and not two people who'd just met. As much as Boone's soul soared, though, his hopes sank. Would Nina take his hand and trust him if she knew about his wolf half?

"Hello, miss," the valet said, flashing her a genuine smile.

"Hello, Toby," Nina said when he held the door open for her. "Thank you."

She was playing her part well, but her grip on Boone's hand grew so tight, he winced.

The lobby was blindingly white with more mirrors than the Palace of Versailles, and a giant chandelier glittered overhead.

"Ah, miss. So good to see you again," a uniformed attendant said the second they walked through the door. "I didn't see you go out earlier."

Boone scrutinized the man for some hint of wrongdoing — a *Holy shit, you're alive* twitch of the eye or a *Let me call the mafia boss right now* clench of his fist. But, no — nothing, making Boone think the man was genuine.

"Oh, uh..." Nina mumbled. "I left early."

The man gave Boone a side-eyed look of mistrust, which convinced Boone the man was all right. He wouldn't trust a guy like himself with a girl like Nina, either. She deserved better. Richer. More ambitious.

She deserves a devoted mate. Forever, his wolf declared.

"I'll get your key," the man said, scurrying over to the desk.

Nina took it as if accepting a rat held out by the tail, and Boone didn't blame her. This just got weirder and weirder. Nina was a guest here?

She fingered the key uncertainly — a real, old-fashioned key — as Boone guided her toward the elevator, studying the lobby in his peripheral vision. There were security cameras subtly tucked into every corner. A blessing or a curse? Cameras might have captured some information on Nina's attackers, but they'd also capture Boone.

Nina looked at him with an alarmed, *What now?* look, but the elevator had an attendant, too. The man smiled and pointed up. "Penthouse suite. Here we go, miss."

Nina's step hitched at the *penthouse suite* part, and Boone had to tug her into the elevator, trying to exude *We got this* vibes.

They stood in awkward silence as the elevator rose, dinging through one floor after another.

"Here you go. Have a nice day," the bellhop said when they reached the top floor.

The doors rolled open, and Boone gave Nina a nudge when she breathed, "Wow."

Then he caught sight of what lay ahead, and he nearly froze, too. *Wow* was right.

Chapter Seven

"Wow," Nina whispered for the second time.

She made it two steps out of the elevator before stuttering to a halt and looking around. They'd stepped into a spacious foyer with a round table and a huge bouquet of tropical flowers — a foyer that opened directly into the most luxurious apartment she had ever seen. Not that she'd seen many, but she'd leafed through the pages of magazines. And, wow. If there were centerfolds for luxury living, this would be it.

That wasn't a wall painted blue — that was the view. An unobstructed ocean view, forming a turquoise strip that ran along a wide terrace that spanned the entire left half of the building's top floor. The interior was decorated in cool grays with burgundy highlights, with a giant screen built into one wall and paintings on the others. Big, vibrant paintings that could have filled a museum hall. A fresh bouquet of anthurium and bird of paradise stood on the entrance hall table, their fragrance tickling her nose.

She turned to gape at Boone as the elevator doors closed. "Is this really my room?"

"Your penthouse suite, Nina."

She shook her head. Her memory was full of blanks, but she was sure she'd never heard her name and *penthouse suite* in the same sentence before. She couldn't possibly afford a place like this.

It was grander than grand, yet part of her longed to rush back to Boone's feet-in-the-sand beach bungalow. That was more her style. Cozy. Comfortably worn. Homey.

"Hang on," he said, sweeping past her. He paused in the entryway, sheltering her body with his, then strode across the room and yanked open one door after another. In the blink of an eye, he'd gone from low-key honeymooner to private body-guard on full alert. His movements were quick and calculated, his steps silent. His eyes roved everywhere, reminding her of the ugly truth. Someone had tried to murder her, but that was on a boat. Did Boone believe there was danger here, too?

She walked to the terrace and braced both hands on the railing — the next best thing to hugging Boone's waist as she'd done on the motorcycle. It didn't bring her the same sense of security, but it helped — a little — as the doubts and fears engulfed her all over again. There had to be some mistake. She didn't vacation at luxury resorts like this. She didn't do anything to attract murders. She didn't—

Squeezing her eyes closed, she fought the panic away. She was here to try to remember something — something other than that awful night on the motorboat. She gritted her teeth, trying to be as businesslike as Boone. Twenty minutes ago, she'd been happily drifting away in daydreams of her and Boone, kissing while slowly peeling off layers of clothes. Now, all the fear and anxiety were back as she looked around.

The terrace stretched on and on like the private deck of a cruise ship. There was an ivy-covered wall on the right where the adjoining penthouse would be. On the left, the terrace wrapped around a corner and opened into a huge outdoor living space with couches, lounge chairs, and a bar. Potted plants with oversized leaves gave the suite the feel of a luxury tree-house, with the tallest palms swaying at eye level outside. The view was to die for, from sailboats bobbing at anchor in the foreground to the vastness of the Pacific — a sheet of blue broken only by the gentle slope of another island in the distance.

To die for. She snorted. Heaven knew she'd come close.

She let her eyes sweep over every table and shelf, trying to think like a detective. If she really had been staying in that suite, she hadn't been there long, because the place was virtually untouched. No paperbacks lying on the coffee table, no bottle of sunscreen by the lounge chairs. No hat, no beach towel. Nothing.

"Nina," Boone hissed, motioning her inside.

He stood at the doorway to a bedroom, every muscle tensed, and when she came close, he took her hand and gestured. "There's no one here, but..."

She peeked into the bedroom and gasped. The white sheets of the king-size bed were knotted on the floor, and pillows lay discarded around the room. A suitcase lay overturned, and clothes were strewn everywhere. The place had been ransacked.

"Do you recognize anything?" Boone asked.

She was about to say *no* when something in her brain clicked, and just like that, the answer was *yes*. Those were her favorite cutoff shorts. That green shirt was the one she'd been so proud of finding at a thrift shop for only a few dollars. And the tattered brown teddy bear that had been discarded upside-down by the dresser—

She cried out and ran over, then clutched it to her chest and rocked it like a baby. She squeezed her eyes tight a second too late to stop the tears.

Boone touched her shoulder gently and whispered, "Are you okay?"

She shook her head. Was the answer yes or no?

"My mother..." She choked on the words. That teddy bear was her mother's childhood toy, one of the few things she'd kept through the fifty-six years of her life. Nina had pulled it out of an old trunk and brought it to her mother in the hospital a month before—

She gulped. A month before her mother died.

"It's April, right?" she whispered.

Boone didn't answer right away. He probably thought she was nuts. "Yes."

Nina rocked the teddy bear. April meant May was around the corner — along with the third anniversary of her mother's death. Yet the sorrow was as fresh as it had been the day she'd held her mother's hand for the last time.

It's all right, sweetie. My time is up, but yours has just begun. Her mother's words echoed through her mind. *Now you can really live, and live free.*

Nina's ears burned, and a lump built in her throat. She hadn't exactly been living her mother's last wish, had she? Too many debts, too many bills. Why so many, she couldn't remember. That was still buried with the rest of her memories. But at least she had this one back.

Boone squeezed her shoulder once and stepped away, giving her the privacy she craved. A second later, she heard him speaking softly into his phone.

"Hunter? Listen, I need you and Cruz here. Right now."

His voice faded as he walked away, and Nina let herself sink into newfound memories for a while. Good ones, like gardening with her mother in their tiny handkerchief of a yard. Sad ones, like reading aloud when the chemo had weakened her mother to the point that she couldn't hold a book by herself. Bittersweet ones, like the two of them walking along a lakeshore with their elbows linked on one of her mother's good days.

Other memories lurked amidst the ones focused on her mother, but she fought them away. This was enough for now. Enough love to last her a lifetime — and enough sorrow, too. Enough wisdom in the echo of the sayings her mother had loved.

Don't wait for a good day. Make it a good day.

Happiness is a recipe you create with whatever ingredients life provides.

Every great journey starts with one small step.

Nina pulled herself together slowly and sat on the edge of the bed, wiping her cheeks. Her mother had never felt sorry for herself; she always soldiered on. Nina tipped her chin up and took a deep breath. Time to do the same.

She looked at her own reflection in the mirror. There she was with the teddy bear in a pose just like one from a photo she was suddenly desperate to hold — the one of her at about age four, with her mother curled behind her and the bear cuddled in her lap. A girl with so many dreams, a mother with so many hopes.

A quiet scuffing sound drew her attention to the doorway, and she looked up. It was Boone, tilting his head at her with an expression that asked if she needed him or preferred some time alone.

And just like that, the little girl's dreams became the hopes of a woman, and she swallowed hard. Boone had captivated her from the start. And just like the first night when he'd carried her so carefully from the beach, his soul called to hers. She'd never felt that around a man. She'd never wanted to trust so readily or to be so reassured. And right now, she needed him. Her mother had taught her to stand on her own two feet, but damn — she sure wouldn't mind a shoulder to lean on.

Not trusting her voice, Nina motioned Boone over, and he sat down beside her on the bed. A slightly different version of Boone — a quieter, more serious one. No wisecracks, no charming smile. Just those bottomless blue eyes, so incredibly sincere. He looped an arm over her shoulders, pulled her in, and pressed his lips to her forehead.

"You good?" he murmured.

She wiped her eyes and nodded quickly. She was now.

He tucked his chin over her head and held her for a good three minutes without saying a word. He smelled so good, she closed her eyes and inhaled, pushing everything else away. Leaning into him felt so nice, she had to fight the urge to burrow closer.

But, whoa. She barely knew this man. What was she doing, weeping in his arms?

"Sorry," she sniffed, forcing herself away, meeting his eyes in the mirror.

"Memories," he murmured, as if he knew exactly how she felt. "It would be nice if we could just keep the good ones, huh?" His smile wavered for a moment, and he closed his eyes, making her wonder where his sorrows lay.

A moment later, he cleared his throat and went all soldier again. "Are you okay to get your things? We need to get out of here soon."

She managed a shaky nod. If he could hide the urgency in his voice, she could hide her fear. Because all of a sudden, she was back in reality. Her hotel room — correction, her penthouse suite — had been ransacked, probably by her would-be killers. Boone was right about moving on. Coming here had been a gamble, and it was time to leave.

When Boone stood, she followed, forcing herself into gear. Boone stalked around the suite like a soldier at a post surrounded by enemy snipers, while she grabbed clothes and stuffed them in a small bag.

"Here," Boone said, handing her the phone. "Tell the front desk to let Hunter and Cruz in."

She made a quick call to the receptionist who called her *miss* and replied to every request with *Of course*, making her wonder what the heck she was doing in a place this fancy. Initially, she'd suspected they had her mixed up with someone else, but the teddy bear proved she truly was a guest. But who was paying for this level of luxury? What was she doing in Hawaii, so far from home?

She blinked as another little recollection hit her. New Jersey. That's where the little house with the creaky stairs she'd lived in her whole life stood.

"I'm pretty sure you don't have to make your own bed in a place like this," Boone said from the doorway.

She stopped, not even aware of what she'd been doing. Then she carried on anyway. At least the cleaners wouldn't think she was a slob, and tidying was her way of wrestling control back from whoever had ransacked her room. When she finished, she packed the teddy bear carefully into the backpack and stepped into the living room.

"What do you think?" she asked in a hush.

Boone tipped his head one way then the other. "They were looking for something. Maybe they didn't want you dead so much as they wanted something."

Nina wracked her mind, trying to think what that thing might be. Then the elevator bell dinged, and Boone whirled to face it, sweeping her behind his body like a one-man army. Nina held her breath, half expecting six assassins to leap out with their guns trained on her head. But when the doors parted, only Hunter and Cruz stepped out.

Well, *stormed* out was more like it, because they both swept around opposite sides of the room, checking every door, peering around corners for potential enemies before uttering so much as a brief hello.

"Should we call the police?" she asked Boone.

He shook his head. "Not yet, at least. Right now, whoever pulled this shit doesn't know you're alive. I'd like to keep it that way."

"How long do you think that will last?" Cruz grumbled.

Nina bit her lip. Cruz was right. Now that she'd been seen at the hotel, it was only a question of time before her would-be killers discovered she was still alive. Would they come back for another attempt?

Her knees wobbled, but just when she thought she might crumple to the floor and go back to hugging the teddy bear in despair, Boone took her arm.

"It will be okay." His tone was determined, the words a hoarse whisper. "We'll take care of you."

Behind Boone, Hunter shot her a bolstering smile, and even Cruz gave a grim nod. The three of them couldn't be more different, but they were a band of brothers who'd been baptized by fire at some point in the past. Men who stuck together through thick and thin.

"Ready to go?" Boone asked.

She'd barely nodded when the men closed ranks around her and stepped toward the entrance as one. It was terrifying yet reassuring at the same time.

"Stairs," Cruz murmured. He took cover before opening the door then pronounced all clear.

Nina had never been in a tank, but heck, she sure felt like it. The men were that solid, that tightly clustered around her. They moved with military precision, scanning the area, barely making a sound. Her own personal Secret Service unit, that's what it was like. No one could get to her in that huddle of muscle. Hell, she could barely see over them. She didn't want to, either, because fixing her gaze on Boone's broad back worked wonders in terms of chasing her fears away with every step.

"Oh, miss!" the receptionist called out when they emerged into the lobby and headed for the front door.

Nina almost felt sorry for the receptionist, because Boone, Hunter, and Cruz whirled and glared. They held their arms out from their sides likes gunmen ready to draw, and she swore she heard Boone growl.

"Yes?" Nina said, trying to assure her self-proclaimed bodyguards everything was all right.

"Those packages that came for you — would you like them now?"

Boone looked at her with a question in his eyes. *What packages?*

She shrugged back. *I have no clue.*

Boone, Hunter, and Cruz stared at each other. It was the damnedest thing, the way their eyebrows twitched and their lips quirked without uttering a word, as if an entire conversation was going on in their minds. A stab of jealousy struck her as she yearned to be that close to Boone, to share that special bond. To be his, and to be able to call him hers.

Just as it had before, that feeling swept her away.

That man is yours, and you're his. It was like an angel was whispering in her ear or a primal voice sounding deep in her bones.

Boone met her eyes, and for a heartbeat, she felt connected to him. Truly connected as the rest of the world faded away. The hubbub of the lobby, the chirp of birds outside. Nothing mattered but her and him.

Then Cruz made a sound and stuck an elbow in Boone's ribs, and the magic faded away again.

Boone blinked a few times as if clearing his head then gave a curt nod. He stepped to the desk with her and looked on as the receptionist laid out a brown manila envelope and a stack of letters with fancy printing.

Nina swayed a little, pulling slowly out of that joyous, dancing-in-a field-of-wildflowers feeling she'd had from staring into Boone's eyes.

"Thank you," she murmured, scooping up the mail with both hands. How was she ever going to get all this home on the back of a motorcycle?

Then it hit her. First of all, Koa Point wasn't home. Second, Hunter and Cruz had come separately, so there had to be another vehicle. But truthfully, she hoped they'd let her dump the packages into the back seat of one and ride with Boone. It wasn't just a cheap excuse to snuggle up against his back, either. It just felt right, the way staying in his modest bungalow felt homier than a luxurious penthouse suite ever could.

She'd just caught his gaze and found the dawn of a warm smile on his lips when a shadow moved behind them. Boone went stiff all over and glared at someone over her shoulder.

"You," Boone muttered as Cruz and Hunter bristled.

They were huddled so tightly around her, she could barely see who it was. She could feel the stranger's eyes on her, though. The dark, piercing eyes of a predator. The roguish smile of a supremely confident man — Han Solo gone over to the dark side, or so Nina imagined from the glimpses she caught before Hunter started hustling her toward the exit. Her soul wailed all the way. Wait. Why wasn't Boone leaving, too?

Boone's gaze met hers, and his eyes blazed in a way that said she had to go. Pronto.

"Wait," she tried, but Cruz boxed her in and hurried her through the door.

"Boone will catch up with us. We have to go now," Hunter murmured. His voice was soft, but his eyes showed alarm. "We need to get you someplace safe."

Chapter Eight

The second Boone spotted his old enemy, a growl built in his throat, and he didn't bother swallowing it away. His cheeks heated, and his fists clenched at the sight of the wolf shifter he hated — the only living being he truly despised. His body and mind immediately went into war-zone mode — blood pumping, senses piqued. Pain stabbed at his chest because he was being torn apart — half of him desperate to stay with Nina, the other half eager to get her someplace safe so he could kill the asshole standing before him now.

What the hell was Kramer doing here?

"Well, now. Who do we have here?" Kramer grinned, showing the points of his teeth. Even in human form, the guy showed his inner wolf. His shit-eating grin and coarse brown hair was all canine, too.

Boone held back a punch — barely — and settled for hustling Kramer to an alcove off the lobby.

Kramer went right on smiling as if pissing off Boone was his favorite pastime — and Boone was sure it was. At the same time, though, the mercenary's eyes darted to the door, catching a parting glimpse of Hunter, Cruz, and Nina.

Boone snarled and let his fangs extend.

"What? Not happy to see me?" Kramer protested.

"What the hell are you doing here?"

"Oh, I'm a guest, of course," Kramer said, far too innocently.

"A guest." Boone made it a statement, not a question, though he didn't buy that for one second.

"Absolutely. I've been moving up in the world, you see. Made myself some good money with the last couple of jobs."

Boone scowled. Kramer had a way of coming out ahead no matter what the odds were, and the end always justified the means.

"And you, I see, have been hired by the lovely Miss Miller for protection." Kramer nodded. "Good idea. Things can be dangerous for a woman in her position."

Every muscle in Boone's body coiled, and the only thing keeping him from going for Kramer's throat was the sound of a Jeep powering up the driveway. Hunter was driving Nina to safety, with Cruz close behind in the Ferrari. At least there was that. But, shit. Kramer knew Nina?

Boone's wolf howled. Kramer had already stolen a woman from him, and hell, the bastard would try it again if only for the sick fun of the game.

Kramer slapped him on the shoulder like they were old buddies and not mortal enemies. "What are we doing standing here when we can get the good stuff and drink to old times?" He pointed to the bar.

"Old times?" Boone scowled.

He, Hunter, and the others had all served their country honorably while Kramer had popped in and out of war zones as a private contractor. Whatever good Boone and the others tried to do — whatever degree of local trust they won — Kramer and his band of mercenaries would come along and blow to bits. War, like love, was a game to Kramer. War was business, nothing more.

Collateral damage, Kramer had once shrugged, deaf to the sound of women screaming in grief.

"Sure. We can drink to the buddies we lost," Kramer said, taking a jab at a raw nerve.

Kramer couldn't care less about losses, while Boone had truly grieved — and still grieved — over every man they'd lost, every innocent life cut short.

Boone clenched his fists before his wolf claws could slide out. He'd rather walk through fire than drink a toast with Kramer. But he couldn't break into a fight here, much less walk away from the chance to find out what Kramer was doing on Maui — and what that had to do with Nina. So he followed

Kramer to the bar on the outdoor terrace and reluctantly took a seat. Kramer leaned back in a chair, taking a corner spot with a view of two bikini-clad women at the pool. Boone sat ramrod straight, clenching his fists.

"What the hell do you mean, things can be dangerous for a woman in her position?" Boone demanded the second the waitress walked away.

Kramer's eyes followed the young woman's swaying hips for a few seconds, and he licked his lips before replying.

"Now, now. You shouldn't let emotion get in the way of a job."

Boone scoffed. "You're the master of that, aren't you?"

Kramer tut-tutted. "Emotions make you weak," he said, putting the emphasis on *you*.

"What's dangerous to Nina?"

Kramer lifted an eyebrow — the one sliced by a jagged scar. "You're on a first-name basis with a client? You know better than that, my friend."

Nina wasn't a client, and Kramer sure as hell wasn't his friend, but Boone bit back his rebuke. The waitress came back with the whiskeys Kramer had ordered, and the second she left, Kramer evaded the question by raising his glass.

"To old friends and new adventures. May the best man win."

The same damn toast Kramer uttered every time. Everything was a contest to Kramer, every venture a way to profit. Boone shoved his glass away and kept his lips sealed.

Kramer tossed back a long slug of whiskey and thumped the glass on the table. "Tamara's here, you know." He uttered the words without missing a beat, landing a direct hit on Boone's rawest nerve.

Will not shift to wolf form. Will not tear his throat out, Boone promised himself, though the effort made him squirm in his seat.

"She'll be so glad to see you," Kramer grinned, turning the screws of torture tighter.

"I bet," Boone managed, though his throat was dry.

The last time Boone had seen his ex-fiancée had been during a short leave between tours of duty. He'd wanted to surprise her, but the surprise was all on him when he found Tammy naked with her legs wrapped around Kramer, moaning, *Yes, yes, yes. Fuck me, wolf. Fuck me hard.*

The exact same words she'd once fed Boone back when he'd been under her spell. He'd fallen head over heels at first sight and told himself Tammy was the one. His destined mate. The woman he wanted to protect and cherish forever. The one person in the whole world who really understood him, or so he had imagined until he'd shaken himself free of her siren-like spell.

Kramer did us a favor, ridding us of her, he told himself.

Goddamn succubus, his wolf growled.

But the pain was still there. The rejection, the deceit. He'd remained faithful to Tammy while she jumped right on to her next good fuck, Kramer — and who knows who else?

A good thing Boone wasn't gripping his glass. It would have shattered from sheer pressure. He'd been so gullible, thinking it was destiny rather than Tammy's succubus magic pulling him in. The woman wanted sex, sex, and more sex — and she got it.

Honestly? Cruz had told Boone when he found out what had happened. *You're better off without her, and she and Kramer are perfect for each other. Two self-centered mercenaries, feeding off each other. Let her go, Boone.*

Boone ground his teeth. He had let go of Tammy, but the scars of her betrayal remained. For wolf shifters, nothing was more sacred than the bond between destined mates, and Tammy had stomped all the faith out of him.

His wolf growled. *Just because she bewitched us doesn't mean destiny won't send us our true mate.*

An image of Nina, stretching and sleepy in his bed, hit him like a ton of bricks.

Our true mate, his wolf hummed.

He shook his head, trying to focus. He needed to put every fucked-up emotion aside and squeeze some information out of Kramer.

"Who are you working for?"

Kramer leaned back so far, his chair balanced on the two rear legs. "I told you. I'm a guest here."

It took everything Boone had not to kick the chair over. He could smell the lie as clearly as he could smell the malty scent of his drink. Just as clearly as he could scent... His blood ran cold.

"Hello, baby," a silky soprano said from behind him.

And shit, he nearly turned. But the words were aimed at Kramer, not him.

Tammy sashayed past, circling behind Kramer then leaning down to kiss his ear. Make that, lick and fondle Kramer's ear. Boone cringed. What had he ever seen in that woman?

She wore a tiny string bikini matched with the Hawaiian print sarong tied around her waist, leaving a hell of a lot of flesh on display in between. The only thing the bikini actually covered was her nipples, and even that was a stretch. Her black hair bounced and curled over her shoulders, putting her cleavage in and out of display, and she stood on a pair of high-heeled sandals that tied with black leather straps, giving a little hint of her preferences in bed.

Every man on the terrace turned and sniffed. Boone would have given anything to casually announce, *She's a succubus. Watch your hearts and your wallets, guys. Better yet, watch your dicks.*

"Boone," she murmured, running her hands down Kramer's chest. Her eyes lit, and her tongue swiped over her lips.

Boone sat perfectly still, worried that the animal part of his body might still react to her.

If I react, it's to her magic, not to her, his wolf growled.

But — no. Not a flicker of arousal. If anything, he felt disgust — a piece of knowledge he held on to like a shield.

Loving Nina makes us immune, his wolf smiled. *Thinking of Nina makes it easy to ignore this evil bitch. All I need is Nina. Nina...*

The sun shone a little brighter, and the stuffy feeling that had enveloped him evaporated with a hint of a fresh breeze.

Tammy's face froze in a crocodile smile as she waited for him to react. And waited, and waited...

When Nina smiles, it's because she's happy. Really happy, his wolf observed.

Boone couldn't help but think the smiles he loved most were the ones he helped create. When Tammy smiled, on the other hand, a thousand warning bells went off in his mind.

"My, my. You're looking good, Boone," she cooed, undressing him with her eyes.

"And you haven't changed a bit, Tammy," he said. It wasn't a compliment.

"Ta-ma-ra," she corrected, drawing the syllables out to give them a sophisticated, old-word feel. All fake, which was fitting. "Such a surprise to see you here."

Surprise? He was the one who lived on Maui. What the hell were these two crooks doing, invading his corner of paradise?

"I suppose you're a guest here, too," he managed to say, though his voice dripped with disbelief.

"Sure am. Nice place, huh?" She leaned closer. "Nice big bed in our suite, too. Just think what fun the three of us could have there."

Even Kramer scowled at that one, and Boone couldn't help but wonder what kind of arrangement they had. Did Kramer indulge Tammy in her wild cravings, or had he found a way to keep her on a tight leash?

Whatever. Boone had never felt so lucky to be rid of Tammy as just then, and it made him see Kramer in a new light. Maybe Tammy was fate's way of punishing Kramer, even if he wasn't aware of it.

"Get out on the water lately?" Boone asked as a motorboat cruised by. He focused on Kramer's eyes, and there it was — a flash of devious recognition.

"Yep. Caught myself a big fish, too," Kramer said, wearing a shit-eating grin.

"Caught or lost?" Boone shot back.

The mercenary's even breathing hitched for a split second — so briefly, Boone would have missed it if he hadn't been watching closely for the tell.

"Unlike some men, I never lose anything," Kramer said.

It was another dig, but a clue at the same time, and the gears ticked over in Boone's mind. Kramer might not have thrown Nina overboard and left her for dead, but Boone would bet anything the mercenary knew who had.

He wouldn't get more out of Kramer than that, though. So he stood briskly — so briskly, Kramer's shoulders bunched as if to ward off an attack.

Good, Boone's wolf growled. *Let him feel jumpy. Let him know we mean business.*

A second later, the smooth veneer was back, masking his enemy's face. "Leaving so soon?"

Boone wanted to shove the words back down Kramer's throat. Yes, he was leaving, but only so he didn't kill Kramer on the spot or give anything away. He'd already let too much slip.

"Bad smell in here," he murmured.

Kramer's smirk said, *Is that the best you can do?* And when he raised his glass in a good-bye toast, Boone could read the words on his face. *May the best man win.*

He flashed a fake smile and forced himself to walk off at his usual jaunty pace. Kramer and Tamara watched him go — the hairs standing up on the back of his neck told him so — and he stretched his shoulders wide. When he mounted his bike and drove off, he made sure to give the engine an extra rev in a clear message.

May the best man win, asshole. May the best man win.

Chapter Nine

Nina stared at the pile of mail in her lap as Hunter drove. *Nina Miller,* the envelope said.

Nina Miller was printed across the second envelope, too. She ran a finger across the top line.

My name is Nina Miller. She could feel a slew of memories press at the edge of her mind like tea lapping at the rim of an overfilled mug.

She twisted to look back for the tenth time. She was with Hunter in his vehicle, a dusty, black Jeep with a dent in the front fender. Cruz was right on their tail in a sparkling red Ferrari, revving the engine impatiently. As far as getaways were concerned, Hunter was definitely keeping a pedestrian pace, driving the speed limit and not a tick faster.

Nina craned her neck farther, but Boone was nowhere to be seen.

"He might be a while," Hunter murmured.

Nina forced herself to sit straight. Was it that obvious that she was fretting over Boone? She folded and refolded her hands then rearranged her mail on her lap, unable to keep still.

"Do you know that man back there?" she asked, picturing the big, hulking guy that Boone had shown such a reaction to.

Hunter chewed on his words for a full minute before giving a curt nod.

Well? she wanted to scream.

Hunter rearranged his grip on the steering wheel. "Kramer. A mercenary. Bad news."

Nina's jaw dropped. At least Hunter told it like it was.

"Will Boone be okay?"

Hunter looked at her, tilted his head, and considered his words carefully, as he always seemed to do. "You're the one someone tried to kill."

"I mean Boone dealing with that guy."

She hadn't gotten a good look at Kramer, but it had been enough to know the man was downright scary — and that there was definitely bad blood between him and Boone.

Hunter navigated another three curves before answering. "Boone can handle Kramer. I worry more about her. The witch."

Her? Who, her? Nina hadn't seen a woman. She stared at Hunter, who'd suddenly sealed his lips.

"Police station is right there," Hunter murmured, slowing down at an intersection. "Honestly, if you feel safer going there..."

Safe? She felt safest with Boone. Leaving him had torn at the fabric of her soul, but Boone had insisted when the other man appeared. Having her room ransacked was definitely a complication, and if the mercenary had anything to do with it... Maybe it was time to go to the police.

She imagined how that might go. *Someone tried to kill me. Can you help me, please?*

What's your name, miss?

Apparently, it's Nina Miller. I don't really remember, though.

"Would going to the police help Boone with that guy?" she asked.

Hunter shook his head firmly then studied her long and hard, as if to ascertain whether she could be trusted. "Look, Boone and the rest of us need to keep a low profile." She wondered what exactly that meant, but for once, Hunter went on, uttering more than one sentence at a time. "But going to the cops might help you."

She chewed a nail then shook her head decisively. No. She wasn't ready to go to the police. Not without talking to Boone first.

Hunter drove on in silence, constantly checking the rearview mirror and throwing Cruz annoyed looks. The other man was

74

tailgating, trying to force Hunter to speed up. Nina stared straight ahead, trying to remember something. Anything.

Nina Miller... Who am I?

They were nearly back at Koa Point when red and blue lights flashed behind them. Hunter groaned and glared at the speedometer.

"Damn it, Cruz," he muttered as he pulled over.

Nina looked back in alarm. "Bad news?"

Hunter shook his head quickly. "Just a speeding ticket," he sighed.

Cruz had pulled over, too, and Nina watched in the rearview mirror as a female police officer approached the Ferrari, checked Cruz's license, then continued to the Jeep.

Nina was expecting a stern, *Do you know what the speed limit is here?* but it didn't quite play out that way.

"Mr. Bjornvald," the policewoman said, a little breathlessly.

"Officer Meli," Hunter whispered.

They stared at each other for a long, quiet minute. So quiet, Nina could hear the swell roll across the shoreline not too far away. Hunter's chest heaved up and down, and the officer's cheeks were pink.

"Driver's license, please," the policewoman murmured. She shot a glance at Nina, who did her best to make it clear she wasn't with Hunter for anything but a ride. It must have worked, because the policewoman trained her full attention on Hunter again.

Hunter scrambled into action, suddenly a puppy, eager to please. He hurried the ID out of his wallet and handed it over. Nina pursed her lips. Hunter sure had a thing for the policewoman, and who could blame him? The woman was downright beautiful, with smooth, perfect features that reflected a blend of Polynesian, Asian, and Caucasian heritage. Her jet-black hair hung in a shiny braid that reached to her waist, and when it swayed, Hunter seemed to sway, too.

Classy. Demure. Serene. The policewoman was everything Nina wasn't. Nina heaved an inner sigh.

Hunter and Officer Meli gazed at each other as tongue-tied as a couple of smitten eighth graders at a dance, neither knowing quite how to make the first move.

"If he was speeding, it was my fault," Nina offered. She'd caused enough trouble already. She didn't want Hunter in trouble with the law. Especially not with the officer of his dreams, if Nina had read the signals right.

The policewoman barely looked at her, so focused was she on Hunter.

"Um, Officer Meli? Can we go, please?" Cruz called, tapping his hand restlessly on the open roof of the Ferrari.

Nina blinked. Did everyone in this part of Maui know each other by name?

Officer Meli straightened quickly and handed Hunter his license. "Watch your speed next time."

"Yes, ma'am," he murmured.

Their fingers brushed briefly, which made Hunter's cheeks flush, too.

"Bye, then," Officer Meli whispered.

"Bye," Hunter breathed.

Nina sat as still as she could, giving them a last moment of. . . of whatever it was that was going on between them. Then Officer Meli walked away. Moments later, she pulled away in her patrol car.

Hunter kept both hands locked on the steering wheel and heaved a dreamy sigh. Then Cruz beeped, making Hunter jump.

"Shit. Sorry," he said, throwing the car into first gear and driving on. He thrust his wallet and license at Nina. "Do you mind putting it back in?"

The license was upside down when she took it, and a memory shot through her mind.

Nina Miller. That's what was printed on her license.

I'm Nina Miller. Mom was Margaret Miller. We live in New Jersey. . .

And just like that, a batch of memories came tumbling out. Not everything, but enough to take her breath away. The flowers blooming on her back porch. The YMCA where she'd learned to swim. The walk to the bus stop to get to work...

The moment Hunter parked the Jeep in the garage at Koa Point, Nina hurried to the beach and sat on a boulder, hugging her knees. A shearwater flew past, but she barely registered it. Like the rest of the view, it was there, but her mind was a thousand miles away.

Nina Miller. My name is Nina Miller. Cottage Hills, New Jersey is home, but there is no one there for me.

The sun was slipping toward the horizon, the blue sky weeping color, matching her mood.

Her mother was dead. Her father wasn't part of her life — she couldn't remember the details, but it didn't seem to matter. Whoever he was, he didn't figure into her life. She didn't have any sisters or brothers, either — all that was clear in her mind. There was a sweet old man named Lewis she couldn't quite place, but she remembered that he'd passed away. No one had reported her missing, either, and if that wasn't proof that no one cared, she didn't know what was. She was all alone.

A bird chirped in disagreement, and the swish of the waves said, *You have Boone.*

She hid her face in her hands and rocked quietly. Boone was great, but she was far too fragile to trust her feelings right now. The most important thing was to figure out the rest of her past, right?

But the past was scary. Ugly memories knocked on the edge of her consciousness along with beautiful ones, and she wasn't sure she was ready for either. She wasn't sure of anything, so she just sat there, rocking herself and wishing she could start anew in a place like this. And why not?

Don't wait for a good day. Make it a good day.

She could do that. She could remake her entire life.

Happiness is a recipe you create with whatever ingredients life provides.

Hell, she was in Hawaii. And no family ties meant nothing to pull her back to New Jersey, right?

Every great journey starts with one small step.

Really, what was stopping her?

A wave swirled around an offshore rock, reminding her why. Someone had tried to kill her. Someone who was still out there.

Boone will help. He promised.

The sun glinted off the ocean as she tried convincing herself, though she didn't get far. What was in it for Boone? Hadn't she already imposed enough?

She waffled back and forth, much like the waves on the shore. They stirred the sand into little patterns, only to erase them and start all over again, making her despair. But eventually, after an eternity of sitting on that rock, feeling piteously alone, something inside her soul lifted. Something even more beautiful and idyllic than the surroundings she'd ignored. She couldn't fathom what it was until she turned to see Boone striding down the path.

Her heart leaped out of her chest, and a chorus hit a high note in her head. *He's here! He's back!*

It was ridiculous, reacting like that, and she forced herself to sit still, letting him come to her instead of launching herself into his arms where she didn't belong.

"Hey," he said, climbing the boulder and settling in beside her, nice and close.

It should have made her soul dance with joy, but the bounce was gone from Boone's step, the fight out of his eyes. He looked tired, and his sunny smile was gone.

"Are you okay?" he asked, though the way he looked, Nina thought she ought to be the one asking him that.

"I'm fine. Fine," she said.

His arm was close to hers, and she couldn't help stroking it, hoping he wouldn't pull away. If anything, Boone leaned closer, so she didn't stop. Maybe it was her turn to console him for a change.

"Who was that back at the hotel?" The second she asked, she regretted it, because the little bit of tension that had eased from Boone's shoulders slammed back in again.

"No one," he said, so bitterly, she knew it was a lie. One she couldn't begrudge him given the way she was avoiding her own truths.

She let the subject drop and sat quietly, running her fingertips lightly over the corded muscles in Boone's arms. Over and over until the sinews softened a little. He leaned closer with every stroke, nestling against her side.

Nina sighed. Reality sucked, but she'd give this fantasy a ten out of ten. A moment of quiet togetherness she hadn't been able to share with anyone in a long, long time.

You're not alone, came the distant voice. *You have him.*

Turning slightly, she brought her body closer to his, wanting him to feel it, too. That he wasn't alone, either. He had her.

"Do you want me to leave you alone?" Boone whispered.

An hour earlier she might have said, *Yes. No. I don't know what I want.* But now, her answer was startlingly clear. "No."

Hell, no was more like it. She took his arm and hugged it, needing something to hold on to. Something even better than a teddy bear.

The sunshine warmed the loneliness right out of her, and she closed her eyes, relishing the inner peace Boone gave her. And before long, she went from stroking Boone's near arm to stroking the far arm, reaching across his body to do so. Invisible energy started crackling between them, and her body heated slowly. She fell into a dreamlike state, tuning in to the subtle signals coming from Boone. The slight twist in his body as he turned closer to her. The heat pouring from his side, inviting her in. The soft, easy breaths that told her he felt better, too.

It was peaceful. Easy. Natural.

Without thinking, she cupped his cheek and stroked it with her thumb in slow, even strokes — the way her mother used to do after a nightmare shook Nina out of sleep. Which was fitting because that was exactly how she felt now. Her skin might still tingle from the panic of the nightmare, but the fear was past, and she was all right again.

When Boone started touching her, too, Nina wanted to purr. The line of palms sheltering them from the rest of the estate was like a wall against reality, and she would gladly allow fantasy to rule for a while longer. And it did, right up to the point that Boone turned, angled his head, and kissed her.

She opened her eyes and found a sea of blue shining at her, as pure and bright as anything she'd ever seen. And, oh — that wasn't the sea but Boone's eyes, soaking her in. Asking an unspoken question. Did she want another kiss?

Yes. Yes, she did.

She nestled closer, slipping her hand from his cheek to his neck, where his pulse skipped. Boone tugged her closer, and she opened to his kiss. He tasted like sunshine and coconut, and his lips were pillow-soft. The longer she held the kiss, the more insistent that primal sound grew.

This is right. This is good.

It did feel just right. And good — incredibly good. She savored his salt scent, his rich taste. The soft feel of his hair between her fingers, the rise of his chest against hers.

This man is yours.

She'd heard legends about gods and magic in places like Hawaii. Spirits, too. Were they talking to her now? Or was it the primal beat of the earth seducing her the way it had enticed sailors in centuries long gone?

Her lips moved against Boone's the way the water pulsed over the sand, ebbing and flowing in steady waves. Taking and giving. Breathing without seeming to breathe, because she didn't dare let go. There may as well have been a bonfire and a row of drummers on the beach, the way her blood stirred. A steady rhythm of arousal she couldn't deny. A rhythm she didn't *want* to deny, because she'd been through so much. Wasn't it time she found something to rejoice over? To embrace with mind, body, and soul?

The skip of Boone's pulse became a gallop. Nina found herself touching his bare skin, pushing his sleeves up to explore. Boone did the same, running his hands under her shirt to touch her sides before pulling away with a sharp breath.

"Nina," he whispered. His eyes were wild. Hungry. Almost glowing — unless she was dreaming, which was totally possible given her state of mind.

"Don't stop. Please don't stop," she begged.

Her lips played over his, and her chest heaved. This was it. A make-or-break moment. Would the primal rhythm win out, or would reality come crashing back in?

"Are you sure?" he asked, dipping his head to suckle the skin of her neck.

An unfair question, given the way it made her nipples stand up, but Nina wasn't about to complain. For once, she wasn't going to deny herself a pleasure as she had so often in the past. The memories were all there — the scrimping and saving, the improvising and making do. There had to have been some mistake at that luxury hotel that held a few of her belongings. In real life, she barely made ends meet. She had a mountain of debts to pay. She—

She cut off the thought there, because she had a man kissing her senseless, and that was all she needed just then.

"So sure. Boone..." She trailed off, not quite sure how to articulate what she wanted. Sex? A lifetime of boundless love? A promise that she would never, ever be alone again?

She knew she wasn't thinking clearly, but sex seemed like a good starting point. She could research her identity later. Right now, she knew exactly who she was and what she wanted. She was a woman drawn to a man, and she wanted him. Desperately.

Chapter Ten

Boone knew he shouldn't go any further. He was crazy to have kissed Nina in the first place, because he wasn't supposed to be necking with a human on his favorite boulder by the beach. But the kiss came out of nowhere — a little like Nina had, that first night he'd found her — and once it started, it took on a life all its own. A force he wasn't capable of stopping, the way he couldn't stop the tide.

Why stop? His wolf howled and clawed at the last of his resistance. *This is our mate!*

The back of his mind tried to serve up an excuse — something about honor and duty and being a gentleman — but the idea never quite came together, not with her kissing him like that. Not with his wolf yowling away.

She needs us. Can't you feel it?

He could feel it, all right. Deep down in his bones, the same way he could feel a storm building over the Kahalawai peaks.

No need to hesitate.

He was hardly hesitating. In fact, he was already pulling Nina toward this place. But in his mind, he was still negotiating a dozen roadblocks that stood in the way. Like the fact that he really ought to be following up on the leads they'd uncovered instead of relishing how soft and silky her hair felt against his cheek. The fact that he had to investigate Kramer's sudden appearance on Maui instead of soaking in the taste of her kiss. Or the fact that... that...

The checklist slowly faded from his mind, making it hard to remember what he had to do other than satisfy the woman in his arms.

He ducked under a palm frond and pulled Nina against his body, drowning her in another hungry kiss. He'd kicked his shoes off by the beach, and the earth felt cool under his feet. The breeze tugged on his shirt, urging him to toss it aside and let Nina caress. Touch. Kiss.

She wants us. We want her. Need her.

He needed to protect her, not mess around with her. Not at a time like this.

Destiny wants this, don't you see? his wolf insisted.

His step faltered. He'd been smitten with Tammy, once upon a time. What if he was wrong again?

Tammy was totally different, his wolf reminded him. *It was all lust, no love.*

Boone had to give the wolf that one. At the time, he hadn't realized it, but now, the difference was crystal clear. God, he'd been such a fool. But still — how could he be sure about his true mate?

Follow your heart, a deep, ancient voice whispered in the back of his mind. The voice of destiny?

His wolf huffed. *Fine. Pretend she isn't our mate. She's still a woman, and you are a man. So get to it, idiot!*

Boone had to give the wolf that. He'd hooked up with a few women over the past couple of years. Why the hell not? But that was just fooling around. This was totally different. This was destiny, and if he screwed it up. . .

"Boone," Nina begged.

He lifted her effortlessly, and she wrapped her legs around his waist, squeezing her body against his, stoking the fire inside him.

Need her, his wolf said over and over. *Need her.*

In the end, that hunger beat his better judgment by a long shot. Boone found himself peeling off Nina's clothes, then his own.

"Nice tattoo," she murmured, touching the wolf inked into his arm. Then she gasped at the sight of the scar on his abdomen. A souvenir from his military days — the closest he'd come to dying for his country. Awfully close, in fact, as the scar proved, because it took a hell of a wound to leave a mark like that on a quick-healing shifter.

He guided Nina's hands away from the scar and led her under the outdoor shower beside his bungalow. Nothing was going to stop him now. Seeing Kramer and Tammy—

Ta-ma-ra, his wolf corrected, rolling his eyes.

—had made him feel dirty and used, and he had to wash that away before getting any closer to the pureness that was Nina.

The open-air shower was sheltered by long vines of morning glory and brilliant red ginger with long, green leaves. The floor was made of smooth local stone. There was always a certain thrill to showering under the sky, a pureness to it, like standing under a waterfall. As if it was just the two of them on a desert island and they had weeks, even months to hide away from the world. But there was urgency, too, the way the setting sun conveyed a sense of urgency. He'd been resisting Nina's pull for too long, and suddenly, he had to have it all.

"Is this okay?" he murmured, pinning her against the wall. His heart hammered, and his cock jutted against her hip.

When she squeaked her approval, his wolf roared.

He held her hands high, kissing her deeply, trying desperately to hold back the full brunt of his passion. Then kissing wasn't enough, and he worked his way down her body, bit by bit, nipping and licking desperately. Her throat was musky with the scent of arousal. Her collarbone so fine and gracefully arched, he spent a full minute there. Then he slid lower, over the swell of her breast.

He'd let go of her hands, and Nina plowed her fingers through his hair, guiding him lower. Lower...

"Boone," she groaned the second his lips closed around her nipple.

His eyes were closed, but he swore he saw fireworks. A whole sky full of them, flashing and crackling with power. His body burned with need, and his cock grew so hard, it hurt.

"Yes," Nina murmured, scooping the flesh of her breast and holding it high for him.

He sucked hard, making her gasp, then released with a pop and licked her skin smooth. He turned to the other side and held his mouth open under the trickle of water running off her nipple, gulping it down.

"Right here," he said, guiding her hand to that side, letting her plump the flesh up so he could drink there, too.

"More," she moaned, shivering under his touch.

Boone didn't keep track of how many positions he'd ever tried or how many partners he'd slept with. But he'd never done anything as erotic or thrilling as this. Never. He cupped his hands over hers, flicking his thumbs over the nipples to make them peak, gulping down water like a man who'd been lost in the desert for years.

A lifetime. A parched lifetime without her, his wolf said.

But, crap. Here he was, chasing his own pleasure. What about hers?

She likes this, his wolf chuckled.

Yeah, he could tell from the way she ground against him and tipped her head back.

"Hang on," he whispered, sliding up her body again.

Nina groaned in protest.

"I swear this will be even better," he said, kissing her ear.

"Not possible."

He grinned. "Totally possible. Turn around."

Nina's eyes were hazy, but she turned in his arms. "Now, what?"

He guided her hands up against the wall, coaxing her to open up by nudging her legs apart. "Now I make you feel even better."

"Ooh. I like this," she whispered, grinding back against his cock.

His smile stretched. Who knew his mild-mannered beauty could drop her inhibitions so fast?

She knows her mate, his wolf hummed with pride. *She trusts us.*

He cupped her waist, then reached forward and teased her breasts. Water ran over her shoulders and down her cleavage, and he watched tiny streams divide and reunite.

Nina leaned her head against his shoulder as he slid one hand lower. Her body tensed, but she spread her legs wider, inviting him in.

"Perfect," he whispered, admiring her curves, following them to her most private place.

"Perfect," she sighed, guiding his left hand lower while keeping his right anchored on her breast.

He rubbed her thigh first, then slowly reached deeper to tease her folds. Her flesh was soft and warm, and every line in her body pulled him to the same place.

"Touch me," she whispered, rocking against his hand.

His voice was hoarse with need when he answered. "I am touching you."

"Deeper," she begged, ratcheting up his inner bonfire another ten degrees.

Her slick heat didn't come from the shower, and when he obeyed her command, his fingers slipped right in. Two fingers, not one, that he circled and scissored.

"Boone," she cried, arching against him.

He pinched her nipple and ran his teeth over her neck.

Right there, his wolf murmured, already calculating where he'd put the mating bite. And crap, if that wasn't a reminder of how crucial it was to keep his beast leashed, he didn't know what was.

No mating bite, he ordered the beast. *Just make her feel good.*

His wolf half protested, half approved. *Make her feel real good.*

"Boone," Nina whispered as he pumped inside her. Moments ago, she'd relaxed against him, but now the tension was building in her body. The good kind of tension, winding her nerves higher and higher.

"Yes. . . " she breathed, rocking against him.

He added a third finger and pumped harder.

"Yes. . . "

Yes, he wanted to roar. *Yes.*

What he really wanted was to lean her over and sink into her from behind. If she liked this, she'd love that. But damn, he didn't have a condom out here. So, okay. He'd settle for giving her an orgasm to remember before taking her to bed.

"So good," she cried, massaging her own breasts, circling her hips.

Feels great, he wanted to say. He winced a little, though, because a faint tapping sensation started up in his head. Like someone knocking on the door, demanding to be let in. What was that?

"This is just the start," he promised, whispering in her ear.

He clenched his jaw, telling himself his words didn't carry a double meaning.

The start of a lifetime together, his wolf hummed. *As mates.*

"Promise," she said, suddenly demanding. "Promise."

His chest ached with the force of his heart yearning to seal the deal there and then. He could bite her at the height of her orgasm and make her his mate. She'd never leave, and they could spend a lifetime enjoying moments like these.

He gritted his teeth. There was so much Nina didn't know about him. So much to figure out first. Like what the hell that tapping in his brain was.

Promise, his wolf said. *If not forever, then promise you won't give up on her. Promise you'll do everything to make this work.*

He nodded. That was reasonable enough, right?

"I promise," he said. Then he quit talking, quit thinking, and focused everything on her.

He nipped her neck. Tweaked her nipples. Thrust his fingers faster. Listened to her cry and mew for more as the tapping sound grew louder.

"Yes. . . yes. . . "

Her head rolled on his shoulder. Her body tightened like a spring under pressure. The water plastered her hair over his body and hers. And when he paused briefly, then hammered back in, she shuddered and cried long and hard, totally abandoned to the pleasure inside.

The water gushed over her body, and he looked down to where his hand was locked over her, figuring he'd let her chase the high as long as she could before easing back. But the tapping in his head turned into an explosion, and suddenly, all his senses tuned in to the sound of Nina's voice.

So good. . . Yes. . . Don't stop. . .

A blinding white light filled his eyes as her senses took over his own, as if she had climbed into his mind and was writhing in pleasure in there.

God, yes. Don't let me go. . .

He could hear Nina. Feel Nina. They were connected.

She said, don't stop, his wolf barked.

He thrust his fingers deeper and swirled them around as she moaned in his mind, unaware that he could hear.

Yes. . . Yes. . .

Boone had never seen anything as beautiful, and he'd never felt as connected. He knew just what she needed and where. When to back off and when to pump deeper. When to press a finger over her clit to wring another ounce of pleasure out of her hidden reserves. Outwardly, her body seemed to be easing back from the high. But her soul was hungry for more, so he stretched the pleasure out.

Now! she cried inside. *Now!*

Her voice rose higher, and her body danced on and on.

He circled his fingers, withdrew, then thrust in again while sealing his mouth over her neck.

"Oh. . ." she moaned, slumping slowly.

He caught her around the waist and held her tight. Her high was receding, giving way to deep satisfaction. He could practically hear her purr.

"Oh my God, Boone," she murmured a second later. "That was so good."

I know, he wanted to say. *I felt it, too.*

Which meant he couldn't deny the truth any more. They were mates. Destined mates. He'd never been that tuned in to another person before. Not to the first woman he'd ever touched, nor the last. Certainly not to Tammy. No one. Ever.

Nina was his destined mate.

Tell her, his wolf urged. *Tell her.*

He pulled his lips inward, locking away the words. No way was he blurting that out now. Nina would think he was nuts, and hell, he doubted he could put something that monumental into words anyway.

Okay, forget about telling her. Show her, his wolf growled.

He nestled his cheek against hers and held her tight, murmuring meaningless syllables in her ear. He nuzzled her softly, then harder, working his way from the right side of her face to the left.

"Boone," she giggled, cupping his face close.

He kept right on nuzzling. Let that be the beginning of everything he couldn't yet voice about wolves, destiny, and true love. Let that be part of his promise to her.

Ha, his wolf crowed. *Another promise. Doesn't even hurt, does it?*

No, it didn't. It just made his soul sing. But there was a danger in that, too, and Boone knew it.

Nina stretched in his arms and hugged him, slowly getting her limbs back into gear. Enough that her hands started slinking down his back and caressing his rear. "You did promise that was just the start, right?"

He grinned and nuzzled her ear. "Sure did."

Chapter Eleven

Nina couldn't quite believe what she'd just done with a near stranger — in an outdoor shower, no less. She wasn't about to excavate her spotty memory for sexual adventures, but if she did, she was pretty sure there wouldn't be too many. And, wow. She'd never felt that good in her life. That sensual. That much of a turn-on to a gorgeous man.

Boone puffed against her neck as if he'd been the one to come to a screaming orgasm under her touch. Nina wasn't sure she could reciprocate by giving him the same level of pleasure, but she sure as hell was ready to give it her all.

"So good," she whispered, kissing his ear. Winding her leg behind his, ready to feel him inside.

"So beautiful," he said, running his fingers through her hair.

The funny thing was, his lips didn't seem to move, but she heard the words clear as a bell in her mind.

"Should we go inside?"

"Gotta dry you first," he said with a hint of a naughty smile.

She grinned. Even naked in what might have been an awkward, post-sex moment, she felt perfectly at ease. As if they belonged together. Forever.

The palms swayed in the sea breeze. *You do belong together. It's destiny.*

She shook her head a little. Obviously, that hard an orgasm could play with a woman's mind.

"How about I dry you?" she asked.

When Boone handed her a big, fluffy towel, Nina's breath caught in her throat. His eyes were glowing — okay, probably just mirroring the sunset — and his mouth opened a crack as if she was the most beautiful thing in his field of vision. Not the mighty Pacific, rippling behind her. Not the lush tropical garden all around, chirping with hidden life. Not the colors of the setting sun, splitting into shades of orange and red. Her. She was the beautiful part of that scene.

She pulled the towel slowly, and Boone let it run through his hand, as if reluctant to let go of the magical moment. Then she smiled and circled her finger in the air.

"Turn around."

He arched an eyebrow in a question.

"The better to kiss you. Touch you. Explore you," she murmured, channeling her inner vixen.

"You're like the big, bad wolf," he commented, grinning at some inside joke.

"Ha. That would be you, mister. Now turn around."

His smile stretched — definitely the naughty beach dude now — and he complied. Nina took a deep breath. With a back that broad, where should she start? She spread the towel and wiped the water from his shoulders. A damn shame, in a way, because the beads of water highlighted every thick line of muscle. Then again, she did get to trace every inch of him over and over again.

"Still wet, huh?" he chuckled a minute later when she was still at it.

"I don't want you dripping water all over the house."

They both laughed. His cottage was hardly a prim, tidy place. The floor was strewn with sand, not to mention wayward leaves blown in by the wind. But that's what she loved about the place. And in Hawaii, unlike New Jersey, you could get away with that. Being inside Boone's home still felt like outside, like part of the landscape.

She worked the towel lower, following the slabs of his lats to his lower back. When she smoothed the towel over his firm ass, she couldn't help imagining all that power helping him thrust into her again and again.

Boone's nostrils flared. Was he imagining the same thing?

She draped the towel around his hips and reached forward to stroke — er, dry — his cock. It stood at attention, and she gulped hard. Would he even fit inside her?

Then she remembered how easily she'd stretched under his fingers and decided she couldn't wait to find out.

Boone put his hand over hers and helped her find the perfect rhythm of up and down. Slow on the downstroke, faster on the return. A little like the water sliding over the sand — a forward rush, then the slow trickle back to the source. She repeated the motion, holding her thumb at the cleft of his cock until she'd stroked far enough away that her fingers couldn't spread any farther. Boone tucked his chin, either watching or closing his eyes to concentrate on the sensation.

Nina watched in wonder, amazed at herself and at him. When had she ever felt the confidence to handle a man this way? When had she devoted so much time to relishing every inch of such a toned body? Sex had always been something she did in the dark, and it was never quite as good as people made it out to be.

Except now. With Boone, the pleasure stretched on and on, and she was every bit his equal in determining what step to take next. Like suckling on his shoulder as she pressed her breasts flat against his back. Scraping her body up and down against his like a wild animal marking its turf. Boone was definitely rubbing off on her in his little quirks, and once again, she was tempted to toss the past away and start a new life from scratch.

Boone caught her hand and held it still.

"No good?" she asked.

"Really good," he murmured, turning in her arms. "But I don't want to come anywhere but inside you."

His voice was raw and hungry, and his eyes shone.

Nina's jaw swung open. Was he really talking about her and not some goddess of the night?

"Let's go inside," he said, pulling the towel from her hands.

"Okay," she managed, which would have translated to *Yes, lay me on your mattress and love me hard, baby* if she could have worked that many syllables off her tongue.

Boone slipped an arm around her, and they turned to the bungalow. Up the four stairs, through the wide-open doors, and over to the bed, where he leaned her back exactly as she'd imagined. She scooched backward to give him space and lay there, open to his feasting eyes.

"Coming, mister?" she joked, hoping he liked what he saw.

"Got to enjoy the view first." His voice was all gritty and hard.

Nina's pulse skipped. That was plain old her, turning him on. And if he liked the sight of her laid out like that, he'd probably enjoy watching her a little longer.

She ran her hands slowly over her belly and toward her breasts, watching Boone closely. His eyes sparkled, so she continued, cupping both breasts and holding them toward him.

Boone's mouth cracked open, and he licked his lips. Lips she wanted on her body very soon. But teasing felt good, too. Uncharted territory for her, but every touch, every action felt natural. Spontaneous. Right.

"You like the view?" she whispered, letting her knees fall apart.

His Adam's apple bobbed.

"I'll take that as a yes," she chuckled.

She circled her right nipple with one hand while reaching down with her left hand, touching herself. Opening her folds, feeling the slick heat that let her fingers glide so smoothly.

Boone touched his cock, making it so easy to imagine him sliding inside.

Nina slowed down, then sped up, and every time she did, Boone matched her pace. His gaze was sharp, his facial muscles set hard.

Nina circled her core and her breast at the same time, wondering how far she could take this. Wondering how far she *wanted* to take this. She was already panting and moaning inside. More ready that she'd ever been to have a man touch her. Take her, even.

"Boone," she whispered, sliding her hands back to her breasts, then stretching back. Giving herself over to him completely, knowing his touch would be better than her own. "Touch me. Come to me. Please."

His jaw pulsed as he watched her, and she had the distinct impression of a predator in the split second before a chase. Holding his breath, every muscle coiled. And a second later—

He dropped over her and captured her lips in a wild, out-of-control kiss. He consumed her. Dominated her. Savored her, moving quickly down her body in a series of hot kisses to her neck, nipples, and belly, where he paused.

Nina threaded her fingers in his thick hair and guided his head lower, answering his unspoken question. Yes, she wanted him to taste her. Touch her. Drive her wild.

Boone gripped a thigh in each hand, spread her wider, and dove in. The second his tongue touched down, she howled. Her hips arched off the mattress as he held her exactly where he wanted her, open to his marauding tongue.

Her staccato cries turned into a series of drawn-out moans, and she squirmed under his tight grip. Boone worked her with his fingers and tongue, making every contact a different flavor of ecstasy. The insistent push of his tongue against her clit, the circling of his index finger. The steady furrowing motion of his ring finger through her folds.

"Boone," she cried, so close to falling apart all over again. "Yes. . ."

He lapped faster, pushed deeper.

Nina teetered on the edge of another mind-blowing orgasm, ready to surrender to the rush. At the same time, if she could hold out a little longer. . .

"Wait," she murmured, suddenly sure of what she wanted.

Boone looked up with glistening lips, and a primal voice howled in approval. That was her on his lips. That was her, filling his eyes with animal desire.

"No more playing. I need you inside me," she breathed.

Boone came to his knees, pulled a condom from the bedside table, and started rolling it on. Nina panted with anticipation, already relishing what she would feel. She considered lying back, wrapping her legs around Boone, and letting him screw her into oblivion. But there was something raw and animal about Boone, qualities that had jumped over to possess her, too. She wanted more than passive missionary position. She wanted to push against him as he came inside her. And the way he'd touched her in the shower told her exactly what they both needed just then.

She rolled, giving him her back.

"Like this," she whispered, coming up on her knees and showing her ass. Wiggling it, begging for his touch.

She looked over her shoulder. Boone's eyes widened, and he stopped in surprise. A moment later, his eyes flashed, and he unrolled the rest of the condom and clambered closer.

"How is it that you can read my mind, woman?" His voice was a deep growl.

Nina grinned. "Funny, I was going to ask you that."

Boone's hands clamped over her hips, tugging her back until she felt the jut of his cock. He was hard and erect, and she whimpered.

"Boone..."

With one smooth push, he was inside her, stretching her to the limit. Tears filled her eyes, stinging her the way his entry had. But her body craved the pleasure that came with the pain, and she urged him on.

"Keep going..."

Boone withdrew then pushed in deeper. Nina cried out in elation, though the pillow muffled the sound. She buried her face in it, focusing everything on the sensation of Boone gliding in and out of her body like a machine.

More, she wanted to beg. *Harder.*

Boone held her hips so hard, his nails scratched her skin, pounding into her again and again.

Deeper, she breathed.

His thrusts were so powerful, she had to brace her arms to keep from moving up the bed. The next time he pushed forward, she bucked back, and they slammed together, harder than ever.

"Nina," Boone groaned.

She squeezed her inner muscles around him, clenching and releasing in time with his thrusts.

"Yes... yes..." she chanted to the rhythm they fell into. Passion might make her blind, but not deaf. She heard Boone's lusty pants against her back. The slap of his balls against her skin. The echo of each one of her cries. And deep inside, that voice that urged her on.

This man is yours. Bond with him. Love him. Hold him.

Oh, she'd hold him, all right. Just as soon as they both succumbed to the tsunami of pleasure that was about to sweep them away.

He needs you, and you need him.

"Boone," she moaned, pushing back harder.

She did need Boone — not just for this incredible pleasure, and not just to protect her from the evil in the world. She needed him to feel complete. To be able to celebrate life.

"Now," she cried, looking over her shoulder. Tensing every muscle.

Boone withdrew, hesitated for a split second, then buried himself to the hilt. He threw his head back in a silent howl and went stiff all over as he released inside her.

Her mind exploded with light, and her blood heated. Her body shuddered uncontrollably as she rode out the high, stretching it out. Her orgasm came in waves, and Boone anticipated each new peak, pulling her closer to feel the breadth of his cock. He read her like a book, helping her eke out every last bit of the high.

A vague memory of another man tumbled through Nina's mind. A man who grunted in selfish satisfaction and released her the second he'd had his fill. A man nothing like Boone. She shoved the image away — far away. Why dwell on that when she could focus on Boone, whispering in her ear and caressing her hips?

"So good," he murmured, easing her sideways until they lay spooned together. He clutched her to his chest and ran his fingers lightly over her collarbone. "Did I tell you how beautiful you are?"

Nina's chest heaved with a sweet sigh. "Maybe you can tell me again."

"You are the most beautiful woman in the world. You make my wolf sing."

She giggled. "Your what?"

Boone stiffened then moved quickly. "My wolf."

He pointed to the tattoo on his arm and studied her closely, as if waiting for some tell. Did the wolf represent his soul? His past? Loneliness? She gave up trying to interpret it a second later, melting at the sweetness of his sentiment.

"Well, if I had a wolf, you'd make it sing, too," she replied, snuggling closer.

He murmured in such a low voice, she barely caught the words. "Bet your ass I would."

She play-slapped his hand, then curled her fingers around it. "Is that a promise?"

She was joking, but his voice was dead serious. "I promise. I swear I do."

She nearly turned to face him, but she didn't have it in her just then. Her mind was shutting down quickly, and all she wanted was to drift away in the heaven of Boone's embrace.

Chapter Twelve

Nina didn't just drift away for a little while. She slept a solid two hours, ate the snack Boone brought her, and followed that up with another round of incredible sex before crashing for the rest of the night. Either Boone's intensity had worn her out, or she really wasn't ready to face her past.

Eventually, though, the sun rose, and even the curtains flapping lazily in the breeze couldn't coax her back to sleep. She dragged herself out of the paradise of Boone's bed and took a deep breath before joining her lover on the porch, wrapping a sarong around her as she went. Would the amazing connection she'd felt last night turn into an awkward morning? Or were they bonded on a deeper level as she so desperately wanted to believe?

Boone sat on the top stair, looking over the sea. When she joined him, he lifted his arm and snuggled her close. So, no, the magic wasn't gone. The kiss he planted on her forehead was soft and tender, but his brow was furrowed, his shoulders tight. He ran his fingers over her forearm, then gripped her hand and brought it to his lips.

"Best night ever," he murmured, kissing her knuckles.

Nina's heart melted all over again.

"Best night ever," she agreed. If only she could say the same about the coming day. Something told her it would be a doozy. But surely she could get through anything with Boone at her side?

He handed her his mug of coffee, and she took a sip, savoring the momentary peace. Maybe she and Boone had been lovers in a former life. He felt that familiar, that much a part of her life. Maybe the past she couldn't remember was actually ten blissful years spent with him. Tracing the lines of his hand, she wondered what life might dish up to her next. Another great find, like Boone, or a crushing blow?

"Well," she said, trying to sound resolute. "I guess it's time to find out who I am."

Boone surprised her by shaking his head. "I already know who you are."

She froze. Had he snuck out while she was sleeping and looked up her name? Had he opened the mail she'd received at the hotel and found a host of terrible secrets?

But Boone just shrugged and kissed her again. "You're Nina, and you're generous. Kind. Responsible."

She bit her lip and closed her eyes.

Boone flashed a thin grin. "All the things I'm not."

She yanked on his hand in protest. "You're generous. You're kind. You're..."

He arched an eyebrow, daring her to say it.

She glanced at the surfboards outside, the sea glass in the windows, the flip-flops thrown by the door. Okay, so *responsible* wasn't the first word that came to mind. More like Peter Pan — a man who didn't want to grow up. But that wasn't the real Boone. She was sure of it.

"You're responsible about the things that count, and don't let anyone tell you otherwise," she said fiercely. *Don't you tell yourself that,* she nearly added. If anything was holding Boone back, it was Boone and no one else.

He held her hands in both of his and turned to her, looking more earnest than she'd ever seen him. His lips moved as if to reveal some great secret, though no sound came out. Then he bowed his head and whispered into her hands. "No matter who you turn out to be, Nina, you'll still be you." His words gave her such hope, but then he added more in a strangely sad tone. "And I'll still be me."

What did he mean by that? What was keeping them apart?

But Boone didn't look like he was about to add anything, so she stood and faced the sun. There were mysteries everywhere — in the past and the present. As for the future, well... She'd have to take things one step at a time.

She pulled some clothes out of her bag and smoothed her hands over them. Yesterday, she would have given anything to touch something familiar. Now, she was filled with a sense of dread.

"You ready?" Boone asked, motioning to the path that led to the meeting house.

"You go ahead," she said. "I'll be right there." She needed a moment — better yet, an hour — to compose herself.

Boone seemed reluctant, but he nodded and walked up the path. The second he was out of sight, her heart ached. She hugged herself. Was it really possible to feel so connected to someone in such a short time, or was she suffering from some kind of rescued damsel complex? She picked up a piece of sea glass and held it up to the sunlight, watching the color pour through. Red like a ruby. Red like love?

She put it back down and forced herself out the door. This was Boone's house, not hers, and she had to get moving. She walked up the path, telling herself she already knew who she was. Whatever she was about to discover would just be the details, right?

The path twisted and turned, and when she came out on the lawn by the *akule hale* — the meeting house — she paused.

Shit. She wasn't just about to face her past. She also had to face Hunter and Cruz the morning after she'd shagged Boone for hours. Could they tell? Would they judge her for it? Did they even care?

She stepped up to the building slowly, waiting for someone to chuckle or give her a dirty look. But Hunter looked up from his oatmeal with the same bolstering smile he always gave her, and Cruz — well, if Cruz was scowling into his coffee mug, that was par for the course.

Boone, though, looked like he'd just been smacked with a stick. He stood hunched over a newspaper at the counter, and when he looked up at her, his smile was thin.

What? she wanted to shout. *What?*

Did she have a criminal past? Did she have three children she'd somehow managed to forget? What?

No one said anything as her eyes drifted to the dining table. The mail she'd been given at the hotel was stacked there, untouched, along with several newspapers and what looked like a pile of printouts. She started walking toward them, then detoured to the kitchen. She could use some coffee first. Maybe breakfast, too.

"Nina," Boone murmured as she rummaged through the refrigerator.

"Anyone want scrambled eggs?" she asked, hiding behind the door. "I'm not much of a cook, but I can whip up some eggs."

"Nina."

"Coffee, anyone?" She held up the pot.

"Nina, you need to look at this," Boone said.

Her hand shook as she poured herself a mug of coffee — excruciatingly slowly, postponing as long as she could. When she finally picked up the mug and set it down near Boone, the spoon clattered and the coffee splashed.

"Darn. I'll just get a sponge," she started, but Boone tugged her back. He angled the newspaper toward her and tapped the box on the lower right.

Everyone went quiet. Absolutely quiet. Obviously, they already knew what she was about to find out.

She slid onto the barstool beside Boone and pulled the newspaper closer instead of following instinct by shoving it farther away.

The article Boone indicated was illustrated with a photo of an older man in a business suit, and the headline said—

A good thing Nina hadn't decided to read the headline out loud. Her jaw would have dropped three-quarters of the way through.

Apparel Industry Tycoon Leaves $50 Million to Waitress in Local Diner, the headline said in bold. Bold and italics as if no one would believe the words if they hadn't been stressed several times.

Boone unfolded the paper, showing her the second picture. A picture of her wearing a frilly apron around her waist and an uncertain smile, with a caption beneath. *"I'm stunned,"* *unexpected heiress reports.*

Stunned. Yeah, stunned was a good word, Nina decided.

She reached for Boone's hand and clutched it as she started reading.

Lewis McGee dies peacefully at age seventy-eight... Attorneys confirm that last will and testament is fully lawful... Family shocked...

Nina gulped. Yep, shocked was another fitting word.

The first paragraph was about the tycoon who had passed away. *Sound of mind and body... A man from modest means who knew what hard work meant...*

She looked at the picture again, and yes, she recognized the man's face, if not the clothes. The image her memory brought up was of a worn sweater and casual pants.

Call me Lewis, she remembered him correcting after she'd started out with *Sir.*

She held on to the counter. Whoa — she remembered! The diner. The customers. The older gentleman who came by every afternoon when businesses was slow and she had time to chat. A kind widower, that's what she'd pegged him as. A nice man with a nice smile who treated her like the daughter he never had. A man who always left a tip rounded up from the standard fifteen percent.

Sweet old Lewis was a multimillionaire? She took a deep breath and blinked a few times.

Boone caught her looking at the date at the top of the newspaper. "This is from two weeks ago," he murmured.

Two weeks?

Nina wiped the tear in her eye and read on. The second paragraph was about her.

Nina Miller, 28... Always on time to her shift, cook reports... "She always has a smile and minute to hear you out," diner regular reports... Graduate of Cottage Hills High School... Mother dead of ovarian cancer, three years ago...

She stirred her coffee and took a long swallow, blinking back more tears. She read to the end, went back to the beginning, and reread the whole article. Then she stared at her own picture for a while, stunned.

Boone slid a magazine over, and she took it with shaking hands. *People* magazine had an article about her, too?

Rags to Riches? the article's subtitle screamed. Nina sucked in a long, slow breath.

The article came with a lot of pictures, mostly of Lewis McGee, his mansion, and his family.

First wife deceased for forty years... estranged from second wife... two stepdaughters...

Black-and-white photos showed a young Lewis beaming next to a woman, while more recent photos showed him next to a different woman in a lavish mink coat. His smile was forced in that one, while the woman glowed triumphantly.

Something in Nina's mind fluttered like a butterfly. A memory of the day Lewis had come in alone, as he always did, and placed a flower at the place next to his. *It's Mary's birthday,* he'd said.

Mary, the first wife. Her birthday was October 22. Nina remembered that clearly. She'd brought tears to the older man's eyes by bringing out a piece of cake and singing quietly with him, then blowing out the candle and whispering, *Happy birthday, Mary.*

The way the old man's eyes stayed on the wisps of smoke from the candle told her what true love was, and they'd held the same little ceremony every year. The man was full of quirky little facts and stories from times gone by, like how you used to have to dial an operator to place a phone call years ago, and how he'd watched steamers glide in and out of New York Harbor back in the day. An interesting man. A good man. But, whoa — a millionaire? Nina never would have guessed.

The article had pictures of her, too. A grainy high school photo taken from a yearbook. Another one of her lined up at a community college affair. The community college she'd been so excited to start, though she'd had to quit when her mother fell ill.

Ms. Miller is unavailable for comment, but sources close to her report, "She's keeping her options open."

Nina snorted, wondering who those sources might be. The more she read, the more the memories trickled back, but there was no BFF or cousin she would have confided in. Everyone she'd been friends with had left Cottage Hills. And heck yes, keeping her options open was a good idea, especially since she had no clue where to begin.

She remembered continuing to turn up to her shift at the diner until the owner pulled her aside. *Honey, don't you think you deserve a break? You have all that money now. Take a vacation and figure things out.*

Vacation. Hawaii? Is that why she'd come to Maui?

"Do you remember now?" Boone asked softly.

She nodded slowly. "The lawyer... Lewis's lawyer said the McGees owned a share in a resort in Hawaii..."

"Kapa'akea Resort," Hunter murmured, nodding at Boone.

She looked around. Of course. Hunter had seen her name on the envelopes. He would have been able to dig up information from there. She scanned the stacks of newspapers and printouts. "You found all this since yesterday?"

He shrugged. "P.I. license comes in handy at times."

She stared at the big, burly man. She thought he was a mechanic. In fact, she had been sure he was a mechanic.

"Jack-of-all-trades, master of none," Cruz murmured at Hunter, ribbing him the way friends do.

Nina looked at Cruz. Was he a private investigator, too?

"So you came to Kapa'akea Resort?" Boone asked, coaxing her on. "Do you remember that?"

She closed her eyes and thought back. She remembered the blinding flashbulbs that had exploded around her anywhere she went for the first few days, and she remembered the lawyer helping arrange a backdoor exit so she could escape the paparazzi. *Just while the dust settles,* he'd said. *I'll get in touch with you through the resort.*

"Do you remember what happened when you got to Maui? Did someone meet you at the airport?" Boone asked.

Nina stood, frowning. "I can't remember." Damn it. Why couldn't she remember?

She started to pace, trying to stimulate useful memories. Not the license plate of her mother's dinged-up car or the name of the cat she'd had as a kid — Paddington — but something that would shed light on her current situation.

"Who would want to kill me? Why?"

"My money's on the wife," Cruz said immediately. "Her and the stepdaughters."

Nina held her head with both hands. "I don't even know them. Why would they want me dead?"

"That old geezer left you—"

"His name is Lewis," she snapped.

Cruz threw his hands up. "He left you fifty million reasons for someone to want you dead."

"But I didn't do anything. I never asked for the money. I'm not sure I even want it."

"Hell, if you don't want it, give it to me," Cruz said.

Boone growled and shot Cruz a warning gaze.

Nina took a deep breath, telling herself to piece things together logically. She all but ran to the table where her mail lay and snatched up the thick envelope with the fancy print. Might there be some clue there?

A sheaf of papers slid out, along with a paperback-size package of some kind. She skimmed through the papers quickly.

Dear Ms. Miller, they all started, and most went on in legalese. All she really registered were a few snippets. Things like *estate should be settled quickly,* or *account set up in your name,* and *all funds should be cleared by the end of the week.*

All of it was dry, impersonal, and focused on money. Things she didn't really care about. She cared about the who. The how. The why.

She turned the package over in her hands. It was wrapped in plain brown paper and tied with a string, like a wartime parcel of some kind. There was a note tucked behind the string, and she pulled it out. The script was long and loopy, the way her grandmother's generation had been taught fine penmanship.

Dear Nina,

There are many crooked souls on earth — but many good people, too. You're one of the latter. Thank you for all your kindness and good cheer. Thank you for bringing joy to the world, one mugful at a time.

She squeezed her lips together, wondering when Lewis had decided to will so much money to her. Wondering why he never told her.

Money can't buy love or happiness, but it sure helps keep a roof over your head. My Mary was never one for foolish purchases, and we saved every cent we had. But when I saw her admiring this, I indulged both of us with one fine thing. Mary didn't wear it out often because she didn't like to show off, but she wore it at home. She said she loved how the light caught the color. If I had a daughter, I would leave her this, the jewel of my heart. So I leave it to you and wish you all the love, joy, and laughter that was in my dear wife's heart

Yours truly,

Lewis McGee

Nina ran a finger over the writing, wishing she had a chance to thank Lewis for his trust.

"You gonna open that?" Boone asked quietly.

Nina wasn't so sure. There was nothing Lewis could have squeezed into that package that could move her as much as his words. When she finally did reach for it, her hand trembled. The package was warm as if it had been left out in the sun. But it had been lying in the shade, and she swore the heat was coming from within the wrapping — or was she imagining that?

Slowly, she untied the knot and unwrapped something the size of a cigar box. Black and shiny, the jewelry box gleamed in the sun. She opened the tiny silver clasp, pushed back the layer of cloth covering what was inside, and—

Nina sucked in a sharp breath and sat down. Hard.

"Oh my God." She repeated the words a few times. Lewis had left her that?

Footsteps whispered over the floor as Hunter and Cruz came to peer over her shoulder along with Boone, who whistled.

"Holy crap."

"What is it?" Hunter murmured, and even Cruz seemed drawn in by the mystery.

Carefully, she clasped the silver chain and drew out the jewel, holding it up to the sun.

"A ruby," she whispered. A ruby almost as big as a golf ball that caught the sunlight and glittered red from a thousand different facets.

"Holy shit," Cruz muttered.

"A ruby?" Hunter asked, taken aback.

"A ruby." She nodded, thinking of Lewis's words. *The jewel of my heart.*

Chapter Thirteen

"The plot thickens," Cruz muttered.

Boone wanted to smack the tiger — for no good reason other than being so unbearably on edge. In part, that was due to Nina being tense and the way her emotions jumped over to him. But also because of what he'd just learned. Cruz was right. Nina had millions of reasons for some jealous soul to want her dead.

She also had millions of reasons to no longer need him.

Money couldn't buy everything, but hell — fifty million dollars? He lived in a shack by the beach on another man's land. His life savings was closer to five hundred dollars than a thousand. Sure, Nina liked him, but really, how long would that last? Nina was a nice, responsible girl, and sooner or later, some nice, responsible man would lure her away.

His wolf growled. *That was Tammy with Kramer. Nina is different. She's special.*

That was the problem. She was special — but he wasn't. He was just him. Worse — he was a wolf shifter, and Nina was human. The shifter world was full of danger and intrigue. Pulling her into it would only expose her to more danger.

As if she's not already in deep? his wolf snarled.

Holy shit, Cruz muttered into his mind. *You know what that stone is?*

Boone shrugged. What did he care about some gem? All he cared about was Nina.

That's no ordinary stone, Cruz insisted.

Well, duh, Sherlock, he wanted to say. It had to be worth a fortune.

Look at it, Cruz hissed.

Boone looked. Okay, a big red stone. A big, freaking expensive red stone.

Feel it, Cruz insisted. *Hell, just get anywhere near it.*

Boone wasn't about to grab Nina's jewel, but he cupped her hand. Nina held the gem by the silver chain, but when she caught it in her left hand and brought it closer to her face, the temperature around him rose by two or three degrees.

It's one of the Spirit Stones, Cruz murmured.

Boone leaned away. Holy shit.

Bet you — oh, let's say, fifty million dollars — that's what this is, Cruz went on.

"What do you know about this gem?" Hunter asked Nina very casually.

"Nothing. I didn't know Lewis was rich."

"He never mentioned it?"

She shook her head. "He barely ever mentioned his wife, and when he did, he choked up."

Boone looked at Cruz. The Spirit Stones were a collection of five precious stones with special powers that had once been owned by a powerful dragon clan. But that horde had been scattered to the four winds centuries ago. And although the stories sounded a little kooky to him, Boone knew better than to doubt them. Kai's mate, Tessa, was the keeper of the Lifestone, and it had protected her from dragon fire.

He went through the stones in his head. According to Silas, there was a Lifestone, a Waterstone, a Windstone. . .

This is the Firestone, Cruz murmured. *It has to be.*

Boone clenched his fist before the shake in it showed. He hadn't given much thought to the Spirit Stones. The Lifestone was one, and it had helped Kai and Tessa fight off the dragon who'd been intent on claiming Tessa as his mate — and that was that as far as Boone was concerned. Tessa was awesome, and she fit right in with their little band of shifters at Koa Point. The place hadn't felt the same since she and Kai had left for their trip to Arizona.

So, no, he hadn't spent much time wondering about the other Spirit Stones. But now, Silas's words echoed through his brain.

When one of the stones wakes, it calls to the others.

Boone stared at the ruby. Is that why it was here? He thought destiny was bringing him Nina, but maybe she'd just been dragged along by fate.

We need to get a hold of Silas, fast, Cruz muttered.

Boone nodded. The problem was, Silas was somewhere in the continental US, tracking down the treasure stolen from his family by the dragon who'd attacked Tessa. Silas had been in and out of contact over the past few days. Who knew when they'd hear from him next?

Hunter rustled through the papers on the table and pulled one out to show Nina. "Look."

Boone leaned in as Nina read the copy of a decades-old newspaper clipping out loud. Something from the society pages.

"Mr. and Mrs. Lewis McGee attending a benefit dinner for the Children's Cancer Fund. Mrs. McGee is seen wearing the Harrington Ruby, purchased at an undisclosed price three months ago. It is said that Elizabeth Taylor lost the bid for the stone once owned by the Duchess of Rothersay..."

"He sent this thing by registered mail?" Cruz asked, looking at the envelope.

"That's the best way," Nina murmured. When Boone stared, she shrugged. "Lewis told me lots of stories, like how the Hope Diamond was once shipped by registered mail to make it look like a plain package instead of something worth millions."

"Here it is again," Hunter said, flipping through the printouts he'd amassed. When he put a finger right on the page he was seeking, Boone was impressed. The bear shifter must have been up half the night, tracking all those articles down.

The article was another obituary for Lewis McGee, and one section was underlined. *Among his assets are a ten-million-dollar Florida estate and the six-million-dollar Harrington Ruby...*

"Six million?" Nina screeched, quickly tucking the ruby back in its case and pushing it away.

But monetary value was just one aspect of the gem, and Boone knew it. *What power does the Firestone have?* he asked Cruz.

Can't remember. Did Silas say?

Hunter looked blank, too, and Boone wanted to shake them both.

"When did you say you got this?" Hunter asked Nina.

She turned to Boone. "Yesterday the receptionist said the mail just arrived, right?"

He nodded.

"I wonder if the lawyer even knows what was in there," Cruz mused.

Boone shook his head. "I doubt it. He was probably just acting on McGee's orders."

"So does someone want Nina dead for the money or the ruby?" Cruz asked.

Nina shivered, and Boone nearly did, too. A Spirit Stone complicated things by a factor of ten. Twenty. Fifty. Humans coveted gems for their monetary value, but shifters revered the Spirit Stones for their powers. Dragons were especially drawn by the legends and mystical aspect of the stones. Silas had suspected that his archenemy Drax might have been behind the fight for Tessa's Lifestone...

Shit. Boone could protect Nina from humans and from most shifter species. But if dragons were involved, that was a whole different ball game. He wasn't afraid to take on a dragon, but odds were, he'd lay down his life in doing so.

I'd die for Nina, his wolf growled.

Of course he would. The problem was, he'd prefer a long, happy life with her. An honorable death didn't have the same appeal.

He hung his head. Maybe a long, happy life with Nina wasn't even in the cards. Maybe he was kidding himself about that.

An alarm buzzed, and Cruz went to check it out. "Someone at the front gate."

Boone flashed his teeth, warning Cruz to be on his guard.

112

Like you have to tell me that, Cruz grumbled before heading off. Boone could practically see the tiger shifter swish his tail, miffed.

Hunter stood and followed. *I'll back him up. You try to get ahold of Silas.*

When Hunter strode off, Boone was sorely tempted to pull Nina into his arms. Did the news change anything between them? But Nina was still processing it all, he could tell. She tucked McGee's note into the jewelry box as if it were every bit as precious as the gem, then stood abruptly.

"Can I get you a cup of coffee?" she asked out of the blue.

A moment later, they both broke into laughter and fell into each other's arms. He hugged her fiercely, more relieved than he could say. Maybe he still had a chance with her. Maybe once he explained...

"I guess the waitress part is in my DNA," she laughed.

He shook his head. "What's in your DNA is your ability to listen. To smile. To make people feel like they count." His heart skipped a little at the thought. She'd sure done that to him.

She tucked her head along his shoulder and held on tight.

"Do you remember everything now?" he ventured.

"Not everything. I still don't remember how I got on that boat that night or who those men were. I remember further back, though. At least, the important things."

"Then tell me the important things," he whispered, figuring it would do her good.

"I remember my mom." She sniffed a little. "I remember my house and the people I worked with. Good folks, really. And the nice neighbor from across the street — Mrs. Lorenzi. She made me a lasagna when my mom died and always kept an eye out for me. I remember going to college..."

She trailed off there, and he held her tighter. "What did you want to study?"

She laughed, though there was no joy in the sound. "Psychology. But I had to stop when my mom got sick. It was hard enough to juggle work and study, and then the bills started adding up..." Her voice faded again.

He smoothed his hand over her hair. "I'd bet you any-thing that McGee guy would have preferred you over the best shrink."

She laughed. "You're not supposed to use the word shrink."

"Tell you what," he said, inhaling her scent. "When you get your degree, I'll make sure I won't call you a shrink."

She pulled back and looked at him with eyes wide in won-der.

"What?" he asked.

She smiled. "My mom used to say that the same way. 'When you get your degree.' Like she really believed I could do it someday."

"I do believe it. Even without fifty million dollars, I would still believe."

She frowned, and he cursed himself for bringing it up.

"I don't even know what it's like to have money. I buy most of my stuff at thrift shops. I clip coupons. I'm not sure what I'd even do with a thousand dollars, let alone fifty million."

"You could finish college, for one thing. And you know what? You can shop at thrift stores and clip coupons for as long as you want." She laughed, but he persisted. "Why the hell not?"

She pulled him back into a hug. "That's what I love about you, Boone."

His ears perked, and his heart stopped momentarily. Did he dare ask if she meant it?

Dare, his wolf egged him on. *Dare.*

"Love?" he whispered, holding his breath.

Nina looked up at him. She caught her lower lip with her tongue, then nodded slowly. "I didn't think it was possible to fall in love with someone so quickly, Boone, but yes, I do. I mean, I think I do. I mean — I know I could be all mixed up. But what else can it be? When you touch me, I feel alive. When you're away from me, part of me wilts and dies. I look at you, and all I want is you. You make me feel good. Happy. Secure. I don't need fifty million dollars. I don't need a jewel. I wouldn't know what to do with it. I just need you, Boone. And that's love, right?"

114

Boone locked his knees before they buckled at the force of her words.

"That's love," he managed. "I love you too, Nina. Ever since the first time I touched you..." He trailed off. Did he dare finish that sentence? *The first time I touched you, my wolf howled inside. You're my destined mate, Nina. I know you are.*

He was still wrestling with words and emotions when heavy footsteps scuffed the perimeter of the building, and Hunter cleared his throat.

Boone didn't release his hug. Hunter could wait.

Boone, Hunter called.

Not now, man.

Boone. Hunter's voice was sharper, and that should have been a sign. Hunter never got riled up. Never. But Boone was so focused on Nina, he let that detail go.

I said, not now.

It's got to be now, man. Kramer's here.

Boone froze. Nina pulled back, picking up on his tension immediately.

"Is everything okay?" she asked.

Hunter looked at his feet, at the thatched roof, then at the floor. Anywhere but at her face. "There's someone here to see you."

Boone snarled and stepped forward. Like hell, he'd let Kramer in to see Nina. *Kramer has nothing to do with Nina.*

Hunter pursued his lips. *Not Kramer. Not exactly. But his client...*

Kramer had a goddamn client?

"Who's here to see me?" Nina's voice trembled. She might not be a shapeshifter, but she sensed the danger, all right.

Hunter took a deep breath and glanced at Boone, then Nina. Why did he look so... sorry? So sad for them both?

"Who is it?" she insisted.

Hunter opened his mouth, closed it, and finally opened it again. "Your husband, Nina. Your husband is here to see you."

Chapter Fourteen

Nina's mind spun so fast, she couldn't think straight. Her thoughts collided and bounced off each other, splitting her mind. She stared at Hunter. He was kidding, right?

Slowly, he shook his head.

Wait. How could he mean it? She wasn't married. She couldn't be.

"But..." she said, turning to Boone for support.

Boone's face was pale, and the space between them turned cold. "Your husband? You have a husband?"

"No!" she yelped. "I mean, I don't remember..."

She could see the anguish all over Boone's face. *How could you not remember your husband?*

She asked herself the same thing. No, she *demanded* it of herself, jabbing an accusatory finger in her mind. How could she love a man enough to marry him and then forget? If she had a husband, he'd been completely erased from her mind, the same way the traumatic memory of getting into the motorboat had been wiped out.

"Maybe... maybe..." She fished around for some foothold on the cliff she was sliding off. "Maybe he's lying. I'd remember my husband, right?"

"It's legit," Hunter murmured. "He's got ID, a marriage certificate, an affidavit..."

Nina took a step closer to Boone, but he took another step away.

"The paparazzi are out there, too," Hunter sighed, dropping a newspaper on the table.

Missing heiress hiding at exclusive West Maui estate, the headline screamed.

117

"Shit," Boone grunted, running a hand through his hair.

Nina's jaw dropped. It was bad enough to have a murderer after her. Now the press was hounding her, too?

Cruz appeared at the side of the building, looking as stormy as ever. "So do we let Kramer and this guy in or what?"

"No," Boone and Nina said at exactly the same time, then stared at each other.

"If we wait any longer, it'll be a circus out there. There are more reporters arriving all the time," Cruz warned. "Silas will be pissed."

Nina cringed. Silas was the broody one who was in charge of the estate.

Look, Boone and the rest of us need to keep a low profile, Hunter had said.

God, she never meant to cause such trouble.

"Let them in," she said in a wavering voice.

Boone's chin dropped, and his chest rose with a deep breath.

Nina wrung her hands as five awkward minutes passed. She didn't want a husband or a ruby or a fortune. She wanted Boone.

She could feel the strangers approach before she could even see them. A dark, oppressive force preceded them, much like the drop in air pressure before the onslaught of a storm. The foliage grew quiet and the birds stopped singing, and when the newcomers appeared at the edge of the meeting house — two men and a woman, flanked by Hunter and Cruz — Nina stared, waiting for the rest of her memory to sink back in.

But there was nothing. She didn't recognize any of them. Wait — the big one with the cruel smile seemed familiar. Something about him reminded her of Boone — but in a twisted, scary way. She cringed. How on earth could she have married a man that arrogant? That mean?

But it was the scrawny guy at his side who cried, "Baby! I've been worried to death about you!" and rushed up to her. He caught her in a slap of a hug that sent her two steps back.

Boone jumped forward to halt the man then stopped cold, looking at the floor again.

Nina's whole body tensed. This was her husband? He reeked of cigarette smoke and cheap cologne, and his natty beard scratched her chin. His hands reached much too high around her ribs, almost touching her breasts. Nina folded her elbows in, wrestling for space.

"It's me. Mike!" he snorted in her ear.

Nina winced and shut her eyes tight. This wasn't happening. Any second now, she would wake up in Boone's bed, start the day over, and the nightmare would be gone, right?

"Happy reunion, eh?" the big, cruel one smirked.

"Shut it, Kramer," Boone barked.

It was Hunter, not Boone, who stepped over and pushed Mike away from Nina. "Do you know this guy?" he asked her in his gentle giant's voice.

"Of course she knows me. I'm her husband," Mike protested. "We were high school sweethearts."

A twitch started up in the corner of Nina's eye. As vile as Mike was, something about him was familiar.

"The beard is new," Mike said, rubbing his chin.

She did her best to give him a fair chance. His clothes and shoes were new, and he kept tugging at his tie. Had he spiffed up for the occasion?

"Got the proof right here," Kramer said, holding up a certificate.

Boone all but tore the paper from his hand and glared. There was definitely some bad blood between those two. And there was definitely some history between Boone and the haute couture model-type at Kramer's side. The woman was striking — tall and thin with thick, pouty lips, though cold and cruel like Kramer. The sultry, familiar looks she shot at Boone made Nina's blood boil.

"Where did you get married?" Hunter asked, studying the papers Boone handed him.

"Atlantic City," Nina murmured without thinking, her attention still focused on Boone.

"Atlantic City," Mike said at the same time.

Nina wobbled on her feet. Wait. Was he really her husband?

"Princess! You remember!" Mike cheered, grabbing her again.

Princess? The word chipped at some stubborn memory that refused to loosen itself from the back of her mind.

"When did you get married?" Hunter asked, checking the certificate again.

June 17, three years after high school graduation. The answer popped into her mind.

"June 17," Mike said, going on about the day, the dress she wore, and how they'd vowed to love each other forever.

Nina felt sick. She really was married to Mike. Bit by bit, the uncomfortable memories seeped back into her mind. But a foreboding cloud remained, harboring dark secrets. Secrets she was desperate to uncover because something wasn't right about all this. Something was terribly, terribly wrong.

She looked at Boone for help, and the expression on his face only cemented that point. There was something terribly wrong, all right. She never should have slept with him. She'd managed to forget her own husband the way she'd forgotten getting in the motorboat.

Out of nowhere, the details of that night played out in her mind.

Get her, one of the men had yelled, smacking at her with an oar.

She shook her head, trying to focus on one thing at a time.

"Get your things, princess," Mike said. "We're going home."

She wanted to shrivel up and disappear. *Home* simply didn't gel with Mike's face. Her memory did serve up an image of him sitting on the porch of her tiny house in New Jersey, but that didn't fit *home* either, because the rest of her memories of the house were of living there with her mother or living there alone. She'd spent the last few years alone in that house. She was sure of it.

"Boone..." she whispered.

He looked at her with the eyes of a trusting puppy who'd been kicked in the ribs. "Yeah," he rasped. "I'll get your stuff."

She shook her head wildly. That wasn't what she'd meant at all. "Wait..."

"I'll help you, Boone," the beauty queen at Kramer's side sang, prancing forward.

Nina's hands balled into fists, but Boone's reaction stopped the woman cold.

"Don't," he barked murderously, right in the woman's face. She faltered and stepped back.

Boone even bared his teeth at the woman, and Nina gaped. She'd never seen Boone look so angry, so hard. A different Boone. But scary as he appeared at that moment, all she wanted was to run over and hold him. To reassure him that everything would be okay.

But nothing was okay, and she knew it.

She watched as he walked down the trail to his cottage. All the hope drained out of her, seeing the final rejection in that gesture. He didn't want her in his house. He didn't want her possessions around. He wanted her gone.

"You guys try to pull anything, and we'll have a warrant for your arrest out like that." Kramer snapped his fingers.

"A warrant for what?" Cruz practically spat at his feet.

"For holding a woman against her will. Kidnapping. You name it."

"Kidnapping?" Cruz cried.

Nina nearly choked on the same word. She was the one who'd dragged Boone, Cruz, and Hunter into her troubles. All they'd offered her was a safe place to stay.

An insect scratched at the thatched roof over her head. The sea breeze teased her bare legs. Nina closed her eyes. Koa Point was a little slice of paradise, and she'd brought the devil in. She opened her eyes and forced herself to look at Mike, Kramer, and the woman. Instinct told her they were not to be trusted, but she had to go. They were her problem now, not a problem for the three honest men who'd gone out of their way to help her without asking for anything in return.

She took a deep breath and looked around the estate one last time. Boone appeared with her backpack, showing her the teddy bear near the top before flipping the top flap over it.

Her eyes grew moist. Boone knew what mattered most to her, and he respected it.

"Damn, don't tell me you still have that old thing," Mike muttered, grabbing the backpack.

Nina snatched it back and clutched it to her chest. "I'll take it."

"Oh. Don't forget your mail," Kramer said, waggling his eyebrows at the table.

Nina froze. The man didn't miss a thing. She'd completely forgotten about the mail and the touching letter from Lewis McGee. And whoa — the six-million-dollar ruby.

Boone and the others froze, too, and she remembered how troubled they appeared when they'd looked at the ruby. She sensed another silent conversation pass between the men. She wanted to scream. How did they do that? Did men who'd been through combat have a way of reading each other's minds?

Nina looked at the black box that contained the ruby, then whispered, "Keep it." She turned to Boone and looked him square in the eye, blinking back her tears. She could barely hear her own voice, and she ached to take his hand. "Please keep it. It's the least I can do."

An animal growl came from behind her, and Hunter tensed, ready for a fight. Boone, on the other hand, took on a softer expression for the first time since Mike's appearance. He took the box and weighed it in his hand. His eyes slid closed, and for a minute, temptation flashed across his face. But then he opened his pure blue eyes, reached to her, and helped her close her reluctant hands around the box.

"It's yours. Lewis wanted you to have it."

Boone didn't say more, but his eyes telegraphed the words from Lewis's letter. *The jewel of my heart. I wish you love, joy, and laughter...*

Boone was saying good-bye. Nina squeezed her lips together, holding back the tears. *I don't want to go.*

Cruz muttered a protest, obviously not pleased, but Boone glared back. "It's hers, not ours."

"Damn right, it is," Kramer growled.

Nina shivered and pushed the box into her backpack close to the teddy bear, keeping it out of Kramer's sight. She grabbed the rest of the mail next, because the lawyer's information was on there, and something told her she'd need it.

"Let's go, baby," Mike said.

Her lips trembled as she carefully did up the straps of her backpack, buying time.

"So good seeing you again, Boone," the woman purred, shooting lusty looks his way.

Nina felt sick. She wanted to chase that woman away from her man, but Boone wasn't her man. Mike was.

"Hasta luego,* bro," Kramer said, pinning Boone with a haughty look of triumph that said, I win again.*

Nina wanted to beat her hands on the arrogant man's chest. *You will never be as honorable or as good a man as Boone.*

But Mike was already dragging her by the elbow, saying, "Right this way."

Right this way, a voice in her past echoed. The memory flittered through her mind, there for a heartbeat, then gone again.

Nina twisted to look back, but it was too late. A bend in the path hid the *akule hale,* and while Hunter and Cruz were escorting her to the gate, Boone was nowhere in sight.

"Right this way," Mike repeated.

Alarms went off in her mind. A dozen lightning flashes blinded her — enough to convince her to pull away. Something was wrong. She shouldn't go with Mike. Every instinct in her body told her so.

But his grip was insistent, and his voice sticky-sweet in her ear. "Now, now. Don't be shy. It's just the paparazzi."

She stared. The lights weren't warnings in her mind. They were the flashes of a dozen cameras. The press was crowded outside the estate gate, shouting questions and taking rapid-fire photos.

Mike grinned. "Better get used to it. We're rich and famous now."

Nina squinted and tried to twist out of his grip, but it was impossible to do that and keep hold of her backpack at the same time.

"Miss Miller, where are you going next?"

"Miss Miller, how do you feel about bring reunited with your husband?"

I feel sick. Dirty. Used, Nina thought.

"I'm delighted to have her back," Mike crowed.

More warning bells sounded in her mind. That wasn't the first time she'd felt sick, dirty, and used by Mike, was it? She searched her memory desperately.

But it was too late. Kramer barked an order for the reporters to back up, and they complied immediately. He yanked open the back door of the black Hummer parked outside, stamped a huge, paw-like hand over her head, and shoved her into the back seat. "Let's go."

Mike piled in behind her while Kramer and the woman climbed into the front seats. Every time a door opened or closed, the shouts of the press changed volume from a muffle to a roar. The cameras fired away, blinding Nina.

More memories rushed back into her mind — so many, she felt dizzy from the onslaught. Memories of Mike, yelling at her. Her, crying back. Her mother, holding her hand. Lawyers, telling her to sign on a dotted line...

Kramer started the engine and put the vehicle in gear, and Mike grumbled, "Finally. We got her."

The lights flashed relentlessly, heaping the rest of her memories back into her mind.

Get her, the man who'd thrown her from the motorboat said.

She turned to Mike, gaping. "What did you just say?"

He smiled a crooked smile and flashed his tobacco-stained teeth. "Finally got you back, Princess."

Princess. She hated him calling her that.

One last camera flashed outside the window, snapping the last of her memories into place. "You tried to kill me," she said, recoiling. "You were on the boat that night."

The woman in the front seat twisted around to scold Mike. "I told you she'd remember."

Nina was flabbergasted. Were they all in on this? She reached for the door handle, ready to leap out of the car, but Kramer hit the central lock. He flashed a pointy-toothed smile at her in the rearview mirror.

"Now, now. Is that any way to talk to your husband?"

Husband. Lawyers. Signing papers... Slowly, the memories arranged themselves in her mind. Mike had been her boyfriend through her last year of high school, though her friends and teachers had hinted she'd be better off without him. She had married Mike in Atlantic City, because she'd been young and clueless, and Mike hadn't started his downhill slide into unemployment and drinking yet. But it didn't take long for him to become a mess of a man, and when he turned to gambling, the debts racked up quickly — debts she'd had to mortgage the house to repay. When her mother fell ill, Mike hardly seemed to care. That was the image she'd remembered on the porch — Mike swigging down another beer when she dragged herself home after classes, a shift at the diner, and a visit to her mother. All Mike had done was demand dinner, and at some point, she'd had enough.

"You're not my husband," she hissed as it all fell into place. "I divorced you." She remembered it clearly now. Having to hand the lawyer a check written for the last few cents in her account had been a slap in the face, but at least it had freed her of Mike. "I divorced you," she insisted.

Mike shook his head. "You tried to divorce me, baby. The second check to the lawyer bounced." He feigned surprise at her look of horror. "What, didn't you get the letter? Oh, now I remember. I took that letter out of the mailbox the day I came to pick up my stuff."

She stared.

"I guess you were at work. Anyone ever tell you that you work too much?"

No, Nina wanted to scream. A person had to work to make ends meet. Her mother had taught her that.

125

"But, lucky me—" Mike stretched and put his hands behind his head "—some old coot dies, leaves you millions, and we're still married." His voice dropped to a threat. "What's yours is mine, till death do we part."

She turned to pound on the window for help, but the reporters were out of sight, the car rushing down the road.

"Aw, she misses Boone," the woman in the front seat chuckled.

If Nina hadn't been busy trying to work the lock, she would have gouged the woman's eyes out.

Mike scowled. "I don't know what made you shack up with those guys. They probably just wanted to cheat you out of our money."

I didn't shack up with them. I washed up on their beach after you tried to kill me, Nina wanted to say, but her throat was too dry, too tight with panic. As for the money, she still couldn't think of it as her own, but it certainly wasn't Mike's. It was Lewis McGee's. And Boone sure as hell wasn't interested in money. He'd only been interested in her. The real her.

"Boone is an awfully good fuck," the woman went on in a bittersweet tone.

Kramer growled. "Watch it, Tamara."

"Just speaking the truth." Tamara shrugged. "And yeah, what woman wouldn't shack up with those guys? I've never slept with Hunter, but I bet he's a monster in bed, too. And Cruz... Yum."

"Tamara," Kramer warned.

The woman just chuckled and teased his ear. "A woman can dream. Right, honey?"

Nina couldn't believe her ears. What was with that woman? What Nina and Boone had shared wasn't a monster fuck — it was a true connection, far beyond the physical. It was... it was...

Destiny, a tragic voice whispered in her mind.

Nina covered her face with her hands and huddled into a tight ball, screaming to Boone in her mind.

Boone, I'm so sorry. Boone, help me. Please...

Chapter Fifteen

The second Nina stepped out of sight, Boone slumped into a chair and propped his elbows on his knees. He scrubbed his hands over his face again and again.

Nina was gone. The best thing that had ever happened to him was gone.

Boone... He could sense her calling to him, but he shut the connection down. Nina was married. She had *forgotten* her husband. What did that say about her?

That man is a worm! his wolf howled. *It's some kind of trick.*

Yeah, well, he'd seen the marriage certificate, and Nina confirmed it with the place and date.

He couldn't get her stricken look out of his mind, and he couldn't erase the way Kramer had rubbed it all in.

Hasta luego, he'd said aloud. Kramer had shot an extra *Asshole* straight into Boone's mind and appended that with a triumphant laugh. *Here I go, taking a second woman away from you, Boone. I guess you can say the best man wins — again.*

Boone clawed at his jeans. He'd been ready to rip Kramer apart, but he'd had to hold back. Nina really was married to that asshole Mike, so he could hardly fight to keep her at Koa Point, no matter how it gutted him to see her go. The press had come down on the estate like locusts, too, which would piss Silas off, and rightly so. They couldn't afford to have humans sniffing around. The estate was their sanctuary, their hideaway, and things were precarious enough as it was. The owner of the property wouldn't reveal his — or her — identity to anyone other than Silas, but clearly, that person relished privacy. Having the press show up could get Boone and the others kicked off what was a pretty sweet living arrangement.

Who cares about a sweet deal? Nina is our mate! his wolf cried.

Boone scowled. He'd thought so, too, but apparently, he'd made another huge mistake. If Nina could forget her husband, she could forget him, too — especially when she had fifty million dollars to keep busy with. Fate was just fucking with him. Destined mates were only a legend, a fairy tale shifters passed around like campfire stories. None of it was true, and he had the broken heart to prove it.

Best night ever, Nina's words echoed in his mind.

He snorted. Yeah — followed by the worst day in his life.

Cruz and Hunter filed silently back into the meeting house. He didn't look up, not even when Hunter poured him a drink.

Hunter poured two more and clinked glasses with Cruz.

"To Nina," Hunter murmured in his deep, grizzly voice. "May she find the happiness she deserves."

Boone's ears twitched. Hell, even grouchy Cruz was in on that toast. He ought to be man enough to do the same.

He forced his chin up and raised the glass, though he couldn't get any words out of his mouth. *To Nina. To the woman I thought was my mate.*

She is, damn it! Fight for her! his wolf cried.

Cruz shook his head. "She's rich *and* she's married. Hell of a way to find out."

Boone sucked in a long breath. Damn it, he'd only focused on his own shock and pain. He'd barely considered Nina. She'd been through so much...

He stuck his fists on his knees. *Don't go there. Don't think about it. It will just hurt more.*

Cruz sighed and leaned against one of the twisted trunks that supported the thatched roof and stared off into the distance. Hunter sat at the table in the corner and unfolded a laptop.

"What are you doing?" Boone scowled.

"Checking for divorce records. Just in case."

Boone's heart skipped in hope, though he knew it was futile. Nina had remembered that weasel, Mike. It killed him to see her go, but a fact was a fact. Christ, did life suck sometimes.

He scuffed the floor with his feet, filling in the emptiness. Other than the sound of Hunter's oversize fingers tapping at the keyboard, there was no sound. The birds had stopped singing, and the earth had ceased its busy hum as if it, too, was mourning. The sun still shone, but the sky was pale and empty. Like him.

Hunter grunted at the laptop and hit a few more keys. "Damn it," he muttered, hitting delete and trying again.

Cruz snorted. "Told you you're too big for that thing."

"You do it, then," Hunter said, angling the laptop toward Cruz.

To Boone's utter surprise, the tiger shifter only folded his arms in staunch refusal briefly before giving in and taking a seat beside Hunter. Boone stared at him. The tiger shifter's family had been wiped out by humans while he was away, and those scars were deep.

"You hate humans more than any of us do, Cruz."

Cruz gave a curt, "Yep."

Boone tilted his head. "So what are you doing?"

"Looking for divorce records, idiot," he said, typing away.

Hunter pointed to something on the screen, and Cruz followed with a click.

"Why?" Boone didn't get it. Why was Cruz helping?

Cruz looked up. "Because we stand together. All of us, right? Even if you're the stupidest fucking wolf on the planet."

Hunter grinned.

"Hey," Boone protested. "Stupid?"

"Stupid," Cruz nodded and went back to his search.

Boone made an annoyed growl, and Cruz thumped the table in a sudden outburst. "I'm doing this for you, asshole, not for me. Because I owe you. Because you love her."

"I don't—"

Cruz ignored him. "Because who knows, you might still have a shot at your mate, even if you are one stupid, undeserving wolf."

Hunter nodded along.

"Hey," Boone shot him an annoyed look.

Hunter shrugged. "He's right. Look at Kai with Tessa. Don't you want a chance at your destined mate?"

Boone ground his teeth. He didn't want his heart dragged through the mud all over again. He couldn't take that. "Destined mates are a lie."

Hunter snorted, and even Cruz gave him a stern look.

"What, you believe that shit?" Boone said.

They looked at each other then nodded. Hunter pointed straight at Boone. "You met Nina — what? A couple of days ago?"

Boone leaned away. Had it only been a few days? It felt like a lifetime. A happy lifetime in which time flew because Nina was there, and she was all he needed.

"A couple of days, and you already knew it was her," Hunter said.

"I thought that of Tammy once."

Cruz scowled. "That woman is nothing but trouble."

Boone sighed. Like he needed the reminder. "The point is, I was so sure about her."

Hunter just shrugged. "Maybe you can't see it, but we can. With Tammy — man, it was like your brain turned off."

Boone made a face.

"With Nina, it was like a light in you switched on."

Boone stared. Was he really being lectured on love by a lumbering grizzly? "Says the man who pretends he's not desperately in love with Officer Meli."

Hunter had been infatuated with the local policewoman for as long as Boone had known him, yet he'd never admitted it or approached her. Why?

"Don't change the subject, wolf. This is your mate we're talking about, not mine."

Cruz's head snapped up, and he and Boone stared at Hunter.

Hunter squirmed in his seat then turned on his fiercest scowl. "You want your mate? Then do something about it.

Or do you prefer to put your tail between your legs and hide from the truth?"

The hair on Boone's arms stood as his wolf jumped closer to the surface. "The truth is she's married."

"Married to some weasel she can't even look at, maybe." Hunter shook his head. "All that shows is that you're not the only one who made a mistake."

Boone ground his teeth. Was Hunter right, or was the bear treading on thin ice? Did he really dare put his heart on the line again?

"That kind of marriage is just a piece of paper, Boone. Are you really going to give that more weight than destiny?"

Boone forced a dry swallow down his throat.

Best night ever. He shook his head. Last night had been a hint of many more good things to come.

He sat quietly as his mind flew over all the little moments he'd shared with Nina in the short time they'd had together. The joy that had come with her arms circling his waist on the ride into town. The way her smile lit a thousand fragrant candles in his soul. The way her voice soothed his soul.

Could it really be true?

Nah, he remembered his cousin saying back when they were both teens. *Who needs a mate?*

He'd thought that for ages, but even his tough-ass alpha of a cousin in Arizona, Ty Hawthorne, had ended up falling deeply in love. The man had been more machine than soul before he'd met his destined mate, but she'd brought out the best in him, helping him become a better pack leader with the balance she brought to his life.

With Nina, it was like a light in you switched on.

Boone took a deep breath, wondering if that light had just gone out or whether he was hiding from it.

The phone beside Hunter started to ring, and they all looked at it.

"It's Silas," Hunter murmured, looking at the caller ID.

Boone swore inside. Had Silas already gotten wind of what had happened? Had the reporters already aired some footage or released news of Nina's whereabouts?

The phone rang again, and they all looked at it.

"Silas is going to be furious about Koa Point being in the news," Boone muttered.

"Silas is going to be furious that you let Nina take the Firestone," Cruz pointed out.

"It was hers. The old guy who died gave it to her."

"Yeah. He gave it to her. You let Nina keep it, and now she's with Kramer."

Boone sat back. Holy shit. He hadn't thought that through at the time. He'd only wanted to do the right thing at a time when his soul was breaking apart.

The phone sounded more urgent with every ring.

"You gonna answer that?" Cruz prompted Hunter.

Hunter considered through another three shrill rings. "I think I might be at work. Can't always hear the phone from the garage, you know."

Cruz looked at Boone. "How about you?"

Boone chewed on his lip. He really ought to. But he didn't relish bringing the wrath of a dragon upon himself. Plus, the minute Silas found out about everything, he'd interfere, and something deep down told Boone he had to see this through on his own.

To prove yourself, his wolf agreed.

Boone sighed. That, or he might end up proving what a fool he was.

Trust your heart, a voice in the back of his mind whispered. The deep, ancient voice of fate.

She's worth the risk, his wolf hissed.

"Are you getting that?" Hunter asked Cruz over the ringing of the phone.

"Hell, no."

They both looked at Boone. *Ball's in your court, buddy.*

Boone closed his eyes. The first image that came to him was Nina, sitting on that boulder by the beach, with the wind tossing her hair. And just like that, his decision was made.

"Move over." He elbowed Cruz away from the laptop while the phone rang on, ignored.

132

His mind clicked into business mode, as focused as he'd been during the life-or-death missions they'd once stormed into together. But this mission he was assigning to himself, and that made it even more vital.

First, he'd have to find out if Nina had ever filed for divorce — to reassure himself, if nothing else. Second, he had to figure out where Kramer was headed and what he had planned next.

"Check the airport," he murmured to Cruz. "If they've booked a flight, I want to know."

Cruz grinned from ear to ear and pulled a blinking GPS unit from his pocket. "Insurance policy. I stuck a tracking device on the bumper of Kramer's car."

Boone slapped the tiger on the back. "I owe you, man."

"Yes, you do," Cruz growled then checked the display. "They're not heading to the airport."

"Where, then?"

Cruz rose to fetch a map, and just like that, the three of them were neck-deep in the mission. Boone paused for a split second. Since leaving the military, they'd all drifted for a while. Him, most of all. He missed that sense of purpose, the structure, the drive the military had given him. Now, he was back in action with the support of the men he trusted most. It was like old times, but it was more than that, because this was the mission of his life. He'd promised Nina his protection. He'd promised her everything would be all right.

You're responsible about the things that count, Nina had said, showing such faith in him.

"I'll give this search engine three minutes, and then we head after them," he told the others.

The phone quit ringing, and Boone allowed himself a tiny nod of relief. It would only be a matter of time before Silas tried again. In the meantime, Boone would see his promises through, and he'd follow his heart. Even if it took him straight off a cliff, damn it — he'd follow his heart.

Chapter Sixteen

At first, Nina hoped Kramer was taking her back to the Kapa'akea Resort. There were enough familiar faces there that she might be able to signal her distress to the security guards, or to Toby, the valet, or to any of the other people she was familiar with. But Kramer drove right past the long driveway, keeping just under the speed limit. He'd even had the gall to give Officer Meli a friendly wave as he drove past.

"Where are we going?" Nina demanded.

"I told you. We're going home," Mike said.

Nina kept her eyes on Kramer. It was all too clear to her who had the control here — the two people in the front seats. Kramer had a barely tamed power to him and simmering, animal eyes. He was so similar to Boone, yet so different. Kramer was the night, and Boone the sunny day. Tamara had a spooky vibe to her, too, not to mention her lullaby voice and sensual moves.

Hunter had mentioned something when he'd driven Nina from the Kapa'akea Resort to Koa Point, hadn't he? *If Kramer's got that woman with him, watch out. She's a witch.*

Nina hadn't taken the comment at face value, but now, she wasn't so sure.

Kramer smirked at Mike's comment and shot Tamara a sidelong glance which she returned with a smile.

A cold shiver went down Nina's spine. They had no intention of letting her or Mike go home, did they?

"Where are we going?" she repeated, staring at Kramer.

"High time you saw a little more of Maui, honey. Don't worry, it will be great."

135

Sure, great. Nina leaned as far back into the corner as she could, her mind spinning desperately. Was there anything in her backpack she could use as a weapon or a signaling device?

She wanted to cry, because all she had in there were some clothes, a teddy bear, and the gem.

Her heart thumped. The gem. Kramer seemed to know about it, but she wasn't sure Mike did. It hadn't been mentioned as part of her inheritance in the magazine articles she'd seen. Maybe she could use it to barter for her life. Alternatively, she could throw it and run away once they stepped out of the car. Worst case, she might be able to use the edge to batter an attacker's face if it came to that. She sat still. Would it?

Crap. Yes, it could. Mike had tried manhandling her off a boat. What was there to keep him from attacking her a second time? Well, the reporters, for one thing. Mike and Kramer couldn't exactly bump her off after being seen driving away with her, right? They'd need an alibi. . .

She bit her lip and decided to assume the worst. The gem was the only ace she might be able to slip up her sleeve. But how would she ever sneak it out of her backpack without being seen?

She started blubbering hysterically, saying any nonsense that came to her head. "Please don't hurt me. Please let me go. Oh God, please. . . " She huddled over her backpack and slowly snaked a hand in, feeling for the jewelry box while she kept up the charade.

"Oh my God, please. . . "

"Shut it, lady," Kramer barked.

"Yeah, shut it, Nina," Mike echoed.

She worked the box open, hooked a finger around the silver chain, and slowly wound the necklace around her fingers, reeling in the ruby until it filled her palm.

"I thought you loved me," she sobbed on, withdrawing her hand inch by agonizing inch. Then she pushed the ruby deep into her pocket.

"You're the one who divorced me," Mike grumbled. He leaned toward the front seat. "How far to the chopper?"

136

Nina wiped her eyes. Chopper? Kramer wanted to fly her out of Maui? Where would he take her? Oahu lay in one direction, and the Big Island in the other, with a hell of a lot of open ocean in between. Mike, Kramer, or that evil Tamara could simply shove her out.

Then it hit her. Kramer and Tamara could push Mike out, too. Mike had no idea who he was tangling with in Kramer. Hunter had called Kramer a mercenary, and Nina didn't doubt it. Mike might have come up with the plan to kill her, but Kramer could turn that plan around to benefit himself.

"Jesus, Mike. What have you done?" she said, not bothering to whisper.

"I have just bought my way to easy street, princess." He grinned.

The corner of Kramer's mouth quirked upward, confirming Nina's hunch. God, what a fool Mike was. And what a fool she had been for marrying him even if he had been a different man back then.

She sat in silence as the car drove down the winding coastal road, fitting the last puzzle pieces of her newfound memories into place. She remembered reluctantly agreeing to the lawyer's suggestion to escape the press by holing up at an exclusive Maui resort. The idea seemed extravagant to her at the time, but it did make sense, and things had quieted down when she arrived. But then a note had been slipped under the door of her suite — a note she had assumed was from the concierge, though now she guessed Mike had somehow snuck in. It was an invitation for a sunset boat cruise aboard a boat named *Angel's Angler*. The note was signed by the lawyer, though she'd bet anything the signatures wouldn't match up if she went back and checked.

She hadn't really been interested in a sunset cruise, but she'd been too polite to turn the offer down. After all, someone had gone to all that trouble for her...

Under her breath, she laughed bitterly. Someone had gone to all that trouble to try to kill her. As in, Mike and the boat captain. She'd had no idea Mike had been on board until they were far offshore.

She'd spent the last days wishing she could remember her past. Now, she wanted to drive the memories away. They drowned her, terrifying her all over again.

Nina, baby, we really ought to get back together, Mike had said when he popped out of the cabin, shocking the heck out of her.

She'd seen right through him. He was only interested in the money. And when she resisted, he'd attacked her and pushed her overboard with the captain's help.

God, if only she had never stepped aboard that boat.

She cut the thought off there. If she'd never stepped aboard that boat, she never would have met Boone. His eyes gave her strength, and his touch. . .

Her stomach roiled, remembering how hurt he'd looked when Mike turned up. Boone had given up on her. She was on her own. The thought made her want to lean over and sob. For real, not for show.

She took a deep breath. She'd survived being thrown into the open sea. If she kept her wits about her, she could survive this, too. Right?

She studied Kramer and Tamara, wary of an "accident" they might try to stage. Once they had the fifty million and the ruby, they would want her dead. Mike, too.

"Finally," Mike grumbled when Kramer pulled down a side road and up to a private drive. The gate opened silently then slid shut once the Hummer rolled in. The metal-on-metal thump of the gate closing behind them made Nina jolt. She was being whisked away to some private property, cut off from any hope of help.

Kramer followed a long driveway then parked in an open space in front of the charred remains of a burned-out mansion. Judging by the overgrown lawn, no one had spent much time at the place recently.

"Get out," Mike snarled.

Nina held her backpack close and slid out, pushing the ruby deeper into her pocket. Now what?

Thick hedges encircled the place, shutting out the outside world. A square of concrete took up the center of the property, where two buildings remained — a garage and what looked like a guest cottage.

"I have to go to the bathroom," Nina tried.

Tamara smiled, but her voice was pure poison. "I bet you do."

"Take her. And keep a good eye on her," Kramer ordered Mike.

Nina's hopes rose when it seemed that neither Tamara nor Kramer planned to follow. Maybe she could get away from Mike then sneak off the property.

Kramer snapped his fingers, and Nina whipped around on cue. "Leave your backpack here."

His eyes glowed, warning her not to protest. Nina stared. It wasn't a trick of the light — his eyes really were glowing.

"Come on, already," Mike called, pulling her away.

She put the backpack in the vehicle, hoping that would appease Kramer, then followed Mike to the small house.

"Right there," he said, waving her to the bathroom. He held the door open and leered. "Go ahead."

She glared. "You're going to watch?"

"Yep," he chuckled. "Just in case."

A good thing she didn't really need the toilet.

"Mike, listen," she tried. "You're in over your head."

"Ha. I got this totally under control."

She stepped closer, shaking her head. "That Kramer is a mercenary. A killer..."

Mike chuckled. "Just what I needed."

Nina stopped. Whatever crazy emotions had made her fall for Mike years earlier had disappeared, but to hear him speak so crassly about killing her...

"Seriously, Mike. Think this through. What's to stop Kramer from killing you?"

Mike looked completely blank. "Why would he kill me? I'm paying him."

She shook her head. "What does he need you for if he has me?"

"You're not married to him."

Nina figured Kramer had other ways to make her sign over fifty million dollars — plus a multimillion-dollar gem.

"Let's get out of here, Mike. Let's run away. I don't care about the money. I'll give you all of it. Let's just get out of here, and then we'll work it all out."

Mike went quiet, mulling it over, but then his head jerked left at a sound. Nina heard it, too — the sound of an engine, whipping through the air.

"The chopper's coming," he murmured.

"We don't need it. You don't need it," she implored. "Quick, let's—"

"Quick, let's what?" Tamara broke in from behind.

Nina froze.

"Nothing," Mike said, total numbskull that he was.

Tamara sashayed over, touching Mike's shoulder. He flinched, then leaned in when she started speaking in a singsong voice.

"Now, honey. Don't tell me you're considering a new plan," Tamara cooed, running her hand down Mike's chest.

Mike closed his eyes and swallowed hard.

"Don't tell me you want to leave before we've had any fun," she whispered, practically licking his ear.

Nina watched in shock as Mike fell under the woman's spell. He leaned into her, sniffing her neck. It was only when he reached out that Tamara stepped away in disdain. Mike stood still, glassy-eyed for another moment before blinking and looking around.

"Time to go," Tamara ordered in a whole different tone.

Mike turned on cue, and Nina couldn't help but cry out to Tamara, "What do you do, hypnotize men?"

Tamara's face split into a crocodile smile as Mike filed out the door. "Something like that."

Nina looked at her with open contempt. "Something like that?"

Tamara laughed. "Sure worked on Boone."

The comment cut Nina to the bone. Of course, Boone had slept with other women in the past. But to think he'd slept with this woman...

"And boy, did that man deliver when I pulled the right strings," Tamara crowed, circling behind Nina like a spider spinning a web. "If he was half as good with you, I bet you enjoyed him, too."

Nina closed her eyes, blocking out the images that hit her out of nowhere — like Boone going down over Tamara's body and pleasuring her any way she bid.

Tamara cackled. "And maybe he didn't find you half bad, either, honey. You've got that lost doe look. He'd be a sucker for that, I bet. Good old Boone, ready to save the world. But you know what?" Her voice dropped an octave, striking an ugly tone. "The world isn't worth saving. Every woman for herself. That's what I say. Right, honey?"

Nina ground her teeth. Wrong. The world was full of bad *and* good. Her mother was evidence of the latter, as was sweet old Lewis McGee. Not to mention Boone.

Boone, she cried in her mind. *Boone...*

"Get moving," Tamara barked, pushing Nina toward the door.

The sound of the approaching helicopter was deafening, and Nina crouched beside Mike with her hands over her ears. The helicopter hovered a foot off the ground, its blades slicing the air. Then it landed, and the roar went out of the engine as the pilot shut it down.

Four big men climbed out, all clad in military fatigues with no insignia, and Kramer greeted each with a slap on the back. More mercenaries, Nina realized as her hopes for an escape dwindled.

She stepped toward the Hummer, and when Kramer whirled, she threw her hands up. "I need my backpack."

He flashed that cruel, self-serving grin. "Right. You get that. Then you get that fine ass of yours in the chopper."

She cringed. What exactly did Kramer have in store for her? The helicopter had been crowded with the four new arrivals, so obviously, not everyone was flying out. Who would he leave behind? And was he planning to leave them dead or alive?

She fingered the ruby in her pocket. It was warm — warmer than her body heat — and somehow, that gave her hope.

"Move it," Mike grumbled.

Nina was about to protest when an earsplitting crash made her duck. Kramer's team immediately went on high alert, spreading out, ready for action. A ripping sound followed the crash, and a Jeep hurtled into sight. A black Jeep with a dent on the front right side. Nina's heart leaped as she choked on a cry of relief.

"Hold it," Boone yelled, jumping from the driver's seat.

Her knees wobbled. Boone hadn't given up on her. He'd come for her, and somehow, everything would be okay.

Cruz leaped out from the back, graceful as a cat, and Hunter unfolded himself from the passenger side and stretched to his full height. Kramer's men were big, but Boone and his buddies were bigger. Her knights in shining armor. Still, there were only three of them, while Kramer had... Nina did a quick head count. Four helpers, the pilot, and Kramer made six. Tamara made it seven, and who knew what she was capable of. Mike was an eighth, but he was like a guppy in a pool of sharks.

"Ah, Boone. Back for more punishment," Kramer called as his men fanned out to circle the Jeep.

Nina rushed to Boone's side, not quite sure what she'd do when she got there. This wasn't the time to hug him, no matter how much she wanted to. No time to explain about Mike, either. No time to think.

Boone solved her dilemma by grabbing her and guiding her behind his body. "Stay right there," he whispered, squeezing her hand.

Never had a tiny gesture meant so much. Not since her mother lay helplessly, communicating love, hope, and spiritual strength with the slightest pressure of her hands.

Nina gulped and steeled herself for whatever happened next. She owed it to her mother to face whatever life threw at her, head-on.

She expected half a dozen rifles to cock, but none of the mercenaries showed a weapon of any kind.

"Back to teach you a lesson," Boone muttered.

Kramer laughed. "I already know the lesson. The best man wins. Me, Boone. That's me."

Boone shook his head. "This isn't about winning."

Kramer chuckled. "You're just saying that because you're about to lose. Again."

Boone made a subtle signal to his friends, and they stepped forward, giving him a second to turn to Nina.

"This is about love. I love you, Nina. I should have seen through these shitheads right away. I'm so sorry. Will you forgive me?"

"Will you forgive me?" she squeaked, holding his hands. "I love you, Boone."

His eyes flashed, and there it was again — that yang to Kramer's dark yin, that animal quality.

He kissed her knuckles and looked her in the eye. "Whatever happens next, you have to believe in me."

She squeezed his hands. "Of course, I believe in you."

Sadness flashed in his eyes, hinting that there was something she didn't know, but a second later, sheer determination replaced it. "You have to trust in me, Hunter, and Cruz. Do you have the ruby? It might help."

Might? How could a gem help in a fight?

"Keep it close, and stay out of the way. Stay safe, Nina. We'll get you out of here. I swear we will."

He spun to face Kramer, leaving Nina to gape at his back. Her sunny, laid-back lover was suddenly more solid rock than flesh. All soldier, bent on success.

"We're leaving now," Boone announced.

Kramer cackled. "Sure, you are."

"You going to stop us?"

"You know I will," Kramer retorted as his men stepped closer.

Nina's knees wobbled.

"You know what's going to happen next," Kramer boomed. "You really want her to see that? To find out the truth?"

Nina touched Boone's back. What truth?

"Do you really want her to see you howl in pain — howl, Boone — then die?"

Kramer was hinting at something Nina just couldn't catch.

Boone squeezed her hand again and whispered over his shoulder. "You trust me?"

"You know I do."

Boone nodded once then yelled out. "This is a fight to your death, Kramer, not mine."

"Wanna bet?" Kramer swept a finger at his men. "No one kills him but me. And the woman, we take alive. You got it?"

Nina slipped a hand into her pocket, needing the positive energy the ruby emitted.

"Good," Kramer announced. "I'll enjoy this, Boone. I might just enjoy your woman later, too."

Nina balled her hands into fists.

Kramer made a grand gesture, stuck out his chest, and yelled, "Let the fight begin."

Chapter Seventeen

Nina didn't know what to expect, but the low growl that rose from Boone's throat was not it.

"Boone?" she whispered in the deathly silence.

"Trust me," he said in a choked voice.

She did trust him. She just— whoa. Was Hunter growling, too? She swiveled her head, watching as Hunter rolled his wide shoulders. A third voice joined them — Cruz, who stretched out his snarl in a low, grumbly undertone.

Nina wondered if that was some strange soldier get-psyched thing, but Kramer growled, too, and his eyes glowed red. Blood red, making her skin crawl. She held the ruby tighter, soaking in its warmth.

You can do this, the warmth seemed to tell her. *You can handle anything.*

God, she hoped so.

"Ready for the big, bad wolf?" Kramer howled, stepping forward.

Nina stared as he hunched, raised his elbows, then worked his head left and right like a man squirming from a too-tight collar.

"What the hell?" Mike muttered, backing away.

Nina quaked inside, fighting the urge to run.

Kramer laughed again, but it ended in a hyena-like cackle. His tongue hung out of his mouth, and his jaw—

Nina held back a scream as Kramer's jaw stretched into a long muzzle and flashed a startling row of fangs. Then all hell broke loose, and all Nina could do was press against the bumper of the Jeep and stare.

Boone roared and toppled forward onto all fours, and for a moment, Nina panicked that he'd been shot. His shirt split down the back and fell from his body. His back rounded — his strangely hairy back...

Kramer snarled, dragging her eyes in his direction. Except it wasn't Kramer there any more. It was a wolf. A huge, dark wolf.

Nina stared. She was seeing things. She had to be.

But Boone was a wolf, too, she realized, looking at the tail swishing just a foot away from her. Cruz dropped onto all fours, shedding his clothes in the same violent way, and his skin took on a strange pattern.

Stripes, Nina realized. Tiger stripes to go with his long tiger tail and terrifying tiger jaws.

She didn't move. She couldn't move. Not with a pack of wolves surrounding her — Kramer's men had become wolves, too — and certainly not with a wolf, a tiger, and — holy shit — a grizzly boxing her in.

Hunter was a grizzly. Cruz was a tiger. Boone was a wolf. Nina saw it with her own eyes, but she still couldn't process it.

Do you believe in me? Boone had asked, but holy smokes. She hadn't been expecting this. If it weren't for the ruby shoring her up with its pulsing heat, she might have started screaming there and then.

"Holy shit," Mike said, white as a sheet. He stumbled backward and ran for the helicopter.

She gulped as Boone and Cruz stalked forward. At the same time, Kramer's mercenaries — all wolves — stepped in, tightening the noose around Nina's position. With no space left to back up into, she scrambled onto the hood of the Jeep. The vehicle's open cab offered little protection, but she threw a leg over the windshield and jumped onto a seat to gain higher ground if nothing else.

Growls broke into snarls, and the wolves jumped forward, setting off the fight. Two leaped at Hunter, but the big bear tossed them aside with one sweep of his mighty claws. A second pair attacked Cruz, who jumped to avoid them, twisted in midair, and pounced on one's back. He sank his teeth into the wolf's flesh, making the beast scream and roll. But the most horrifying sight was that of Boone and Kramer crashing in a whirlwind of teeth and claws. Their lips curled high, revealing rows of ivory teeth that grew red with blood. Boone's blood? Kramer's?

Nina hung on to the ruby and prayed.

Tamara stood with her arms folded, observing the battle with an eerie calm. The helicopter pilot did the same, impassively batting away Mike, who'd run up to him, begging to fly to safety. The man towered over Mike, and Nina looked away, afraid of what she might see. Would the pilot turn into a lion? A panther? Another wolf?

Do something, Nina screamed at her frozen body. *Do something.*

She reached into the back of the Jeep, feeling blindly until she found a shaft of steel. The all-too-short handle to a jack, but she'd take what she could get. And just in time, too, because the second she pulled it out, a wolf leaped at her.

She screamed and smashed at it with the two-foot stick. The wolf howled and rolled away. It had come from Cruz's side of the car, and the tiger screamed in fury. His yellow-green eyes glowed with anger, and his outstretched claws scraped five deep rips into the enemy wolf's flank. Nina jerked her gaze away, scanning her surroundings. Hunter seemed to be faring well, with one wolf limping away and the other jumping in and out of reach. Boone and Kramer were locked in furious battle, making Nina wince at the sounds of anger and pain. Had she caused all this?

The air behind her whooshed, and she turned just in time to batter away the same wolf. A moment later, a huge, hulking hand reached down from behind and grabbed her by a fistful of shirt.

"Gotcha, my little pretty," a voice growled.

Nina kicked and screamed, clawing at the hands that dragged her back. The pilot — he'd snuck over somehow.

"No!" she cried, twisting and struggling as the man clamped a hand over her mouth and pulled her out of the Jeep.

Boone roared and made a move to help her, but Kramer immediately attacked his haunches, holding Boone back. Cruz snarled, but he, too, was locked in battle with a wolf, unable to assist. Hunter roared and stepped forward, but two wolves blocked his way.

"Get her over here." Tamara's voice rose above the fray, calling to the pilot who held Nina so tightly she couldn't fight back.

In the blur of action, Nina saw Tamara emptying her backpack — her backpack, damn it! — casting the teddy bear ruthlessly to the ground. "Where is it?" Tamara screamed. "Where is the stone?"

Nina's fingers twitched — the most she could manage in the arm lock the pilot kept her in — but Tamara caught the movement right away. "Give it to me!"

Up to that point, Nina had mostly felt fear. But at Tamara's words, fury rose beside the fear. Lewis McGee had given that ruby to his late wife, and he'd given it to Nina to care for in Mary's memory. How dare Tamara covet that ruby? It wasn't hers, just like Boone wasn't hers. Anger swirled in Nina like a whirlwind, building to a full-blown storm. She bared her teeth and bit savagely at the pilot's hand, making him howl. His grip loosened just enough to let her work an arm free — the side holding the jack handle. She stabbed it backward, and the pilot grunted and fell away.

"Bring it to me," Tamara ordered, snapping her fingers.

Nina had always hated it when customers snapped their fingers, and though she'd always been too polite to do anything about it, she wasn't about to be a nice girl now.

"Never!" she cried, brandishing her steel stick.

Tamara's face went red as she pointed a finger straight at Nina. "Bring it to me, now!" Her voice dropped on the command.

Nina's arm jerked forward against her own will, and her fingers dipped toward her pocket, unbidden.

"Bring it to me!" Tamara screamed.

Watch out. She's a witch, she recalled Hunter saying. And whoa — had he meant it literally? A pull acted on Nina's body, making her quake. The invisible force pushed her hand into her pocket, urging her to bring out the ruby. But the second her fingers closed around the gem, that evil force faded. Nina braced her feet on the ground and clenched the ruby firmly in her pocket.

"I said, bring it to me," Tamara hissed.

Nina all but spat back as confidence rushed through her veins. "Make me, witch."

The word *bitch* had teased her lips, but witch worked just fine, too. Tamara's eyes went wide, and her fingers clawed in the air. But no matter how she begged, screamed, or cajoled, her words had no effect on Nina.

"Fine." Tamara stamped her foot. "How about this, then?"

She motioned to the right, and Nina turned slowly, wary of a trick.

"Nina," Mike cried. The pilot held him in a headlock, one hand on Mike's chin, ready to twist and snap his neck.

"No!" Nina screamed over the background of animal growls she didn't dare cast a glance at.

"Give me the stone, or he dies." Tamara's eyes flashed in triumph.

"Help," Mike yelped. "Nina. . . "

Nina wavered. Mike had betrayed her. He'd tried to kill her. Did he really expect her to give up Lewis McGee's ruby? The jewel of his heart — to save Mike's miserable life?

"Nina," Mike begged.

Nina cried, too, because Mike knew her too well. Tamara, too, had figured her out. Nina wasn't about to let Mike die, not for a gem. No human life was worth that.

She pulled the ruby from her pocket and turned to Tamara, cursing the woman under her breath. Kissing the ruby, she whispered, "Forgive me, Lewis." Then she wound the silver chain into a bundle and tossed it to Tamara's outstretched hands.

"There. Take it," Nina snapped. "Just let Mike go."

Tamara brought the ruby up to her face. Her eyes glowed, reflecting the bloody hue of the gem. "Sure," she murmured, barely looking up. "Let him go, Roy."

Nina turned expectantly, only to see the pilot wring Mike's neck and drop his body.

"No!" Nina screamed, falling to her knees.

"What?" Tamara said in her cruel, teasing voice. "You said to let him go."

Nina held her face in her hands, unable to face the horrors around her. The wolf battle raged on. Mike lay dead, not two yards away. The pilot was coming for her — she could feel his heavy steps approach. When he lifted her off the ground, she couldn't find the strength to resist. Not even when a canine roar reached her ears.

Boone. It had to be Boone. But Boone couldn't help her — he was too busy with Kramer, who fought tooth and nail. She flapped her hands weakly, unable to fight back, utterly devoid of hope.

A chilling scream stopped the pilot one step away from the helicopter, and Nina slithered out of his grasp. She looked up, trying to trace the sound of the cry. The beasts battling each other stopped, too, and all eyes swept to Tamara.

"No!" the woman screamed, staring at the ruby. One hand clutched it tight, refusing to let go, while the other clawed at it, trying to push it away.

"Stop! No!" Tamara wailed in pain, falling to her knees.

Nina crawled away from the pilot, but she wasn't able to drag her eyes off Tamara. What was happening?

Smoke wafted from between Tamara's clenched fingers, and a red glow flared.

"Drop it!" the pilot yelled.

"I can't," Tamara screamed and started writhing. The stone steamed in her hand. Her body shook, and her eyes rolled back as she collapsed to the ground. Flames burst out between her fingers.

The dark wolf — Kramer — roared and jumped toward Tamara. Boone sprinted toward Nina. Her eyes went wide as he approached.

That wolf is Boone. He won't hurt me, she told herself. *Right?*

The blue eyes, the tawny fur, the slight tilt of the head — it was Boone for sure, but he still scared her to death.

Get down, his voice boomed in her mind.

She ducked, and he leaped right over her head, knocking the pilot away. There was a sickening crunch, and Nina looked back to see Boone step away from the pilot, who lay in a heap.

Boone whipped around and snarled at Kramer, who howled when the ruby rolled out of Tamara's lifeless hand. As the smoke wafted away, its mysterious source extinguished, the sun glinted off the jewel, creating a brilliant red light — a red light that reflected in Kramer's eyes as the dark wolf turned to Nina with a furious growl.

Uh-oh. She stood directly between two angry wolves, and Kramer was downright terrifying. Nina scrambled to her feet too quickly and slipped to her knees — right onto the jack handle that smashed her shin so hard, she cried out.

As Kramer advanced, his eyes shifted from her to a point over her shoulder. Boone stepped so close, his breath ruffled Nina's hair. He and Kramer eyed each other with pure hatred in their eyes, the way they first had back at the hotel — amplified ten times. Boone licked his lips once then jumped forward for what Nina knew would be the final fight.

The wolves went right for each other's throats, then rolled, kicking up a dust cloud that quickly settled over Tamara's body. Nina stared. Was Tamara really dead?

Boone drove Kramer left, and the ruby glinted from the right. Nina had been about to run for the Jeep when she spotted it.

Get it, some instinct told her.

She stopped cold.

It's important.

She pictured Tamara, clutching her hand and screaming. No way. That gem was evil. Cursed.

But then she remembered Lewis's note. *The jewel of my heart...*

Lewis had mentioned love, laughter, and joy. He hadn't mentioned evil or some kind of curse.

A shadow moved on the far side of the lawn, and Nina saw a gray wolf slinking up, its eyes fixed on the jewel as it sidled around the raging fight between Boone and Kramer.

Get it before the enemy does. Quick! Every nerve in Nina's body sent the same signal.

Nina grabbed the jack handle and ran for the ruby at the same time the wolf did. Okay, so she was crazy. But there was no way she was going to cower in a corner while Boone fought her fight.

The gray wolf's jaws closed over the silver chain just as she grabbed the ruby, and for one wild moment, Nina found herself in a tug-of-war with a snarling, two-hundred-pound beast. Then something gave, and she tumbled backward. She clenched her hand at the same time, and the hard edge of a gem bit into her hand. Yes! She had it.

She landed on her back and looked up just in time to see the wolf spit the chain out and jump at her.

"No!" Nina cried, swinging the jack handle to smack the wolf's muzzle. The beast yelped and rolled to the side then came at her again — and again and again until the jack handle flew out of her hand. The wolf loomed, three steps away, and her heart stood still. This was it. She was about to die.

When the gray wolf growled and launched itself at her, time stretched and slowed. There was the wolf, flying at her with wide-open jaws. The ruby biting her hand, warming her one last time. The roar echoing in her ears until they rang.

A second roar joined the first, and Nina vaguely wondered if a second beast was vying to finish her off. Then a black, white, and orange blur streaked into view, knocking the wolf aside.

A long, whiplike tail smacked Nina's cheek, and she fell. She stared as the tiger wrestled the gray wolf to the ground. Cruz. That was Cruz.

She closed her eyes as the tiger went for the kill, and when she opened them again, Cruz stumbled away from the wolf's body and padded over to her.

Nina gulped as the tiger circled her, pushing against her knees. Half purring, half growling, it drove her away from Boone's fight.

"You have to help Boone," she cried, pushing back.

The tiger refused to relent, driving her farther away. A huge brown shadow moved in front of her, and she looked up to see a grizzly joining the tiger, forming a living wall in front of her.

Nina looked around. Lumpy shapes lay scattered across the lawn — the bodies of the mercenary wolves. Tamara lay dead, as did Mike and the pilot. The only movement came from the two mighty wolves locked in the battle of their lives.

"Help him!" she cried, shoving at Cruz and Hunter. Her left hand landed in coarse fur — Hunter's thick pelt — and her right on the silky expanse of Cruz's striped back. "Help him!"

Cruz grumbled under his breath, but neither of them moved.

Nina thumped their backs again, to no avail. Apparently, Boone and his buddies had some kind of honor code when it came to fights. But Kramer hadn't hesitated to call on backup. Why would they?

The bear chuffed, which Nina took to mean, *He can do it.* She stared at Boone. Could he? Would he?

Kramer rose to his hind feet for another attack. Boone rolled, coiled, and sprang for his foe's throat. They knocked into each other then crashed to the ground, snarling murderously.

She winced, about to cover her ears, but the snarling faded slowly. The wild rolling slowed, too, though the wolves didn't break apart. They held on to the bitter death. A crimson shadow stained the earth, slowly soaking into the dirt. Nina found herself clutching Hunter's thick fur, holding her breath. One of the wolves shuddered and went still. The other held on, its eyes glowing with determination.

Nina's heart pounded as she stared at the deep blue of those eyes, and her overwhelmed mind slowly worked the information into place.

Blue eyes. Boone. Boone was alive!

He released the enemy's dead body, wobbled to his feet, and looked straight at Nina. A moment before, Boone's eyes had shown pure fury, but now, they filled with fear. Nina stepped forward, and this time, Cruz and Hunter let her go. But why did Boone look so worried? He'd won the battle.

She stopped in her tracks when the realization hit her. Boone was worried about what her reaction might be. She took a deep breath. Okay, Boone was a wolf. Could she deal with that?

Yes, she decided. Yes, she could. Boone was Boone, right?

He swayed, exhausted, and when he crumpled to the ground, Nina rushed forward and kneeled over him with a cry. "Boone. Please, Boone. Are you okay?"

His blue eyes found hers and shone as if to say, *I'm okay. Are you okay?*

She buried her face in his fur — yes, his fur — and smoothed her hands over his sides. "I'm okay. Confused, but okay."

Boone made a snorting sound.

Yes, *confused* was the understatement of the year, but he could explain things to her later — she hoped. Nina popped up suddenly, looking at the others. Cruz was licking his wounds with a frighteningly long tongue, while Hunter sat on his haunches, sniffing the air.

"You guys can change back, right?" she asked, suddenly unsure.

Hunter let out a low rumble that sounded a hell of a lot like a chuckle and swung his head up and down.

Nina fell back over Boone and held him again. She smoothed her fingers over his muzzle and slowly kissed his ear. "Don't get me wrong. I like wolves. I mean, I love wolves." She was blabbering now, but what the heck. "I mean, I love you. I love you, Boone. Man or wolf. But honestly, I'd like to get the man back at some point."

The wolf raised his head off the ground to gaze into her eyes, and she grinned. "The better to kiss you. Touch you. Hug you. All that."

Boone's lips slid into a canine grin, and she buried her face against his fur. The sun seemed brighter than ever, the world peaceful if only for this one fleeting moment. The ruby warmed her pocket, posing questions she refused to face at that moment, because all that mattered was Boone.

"Boone," she whispered again and again, gently stroking his fur.

Chapter Eighteen

Boone pushed his weary head against Nina's hand. His tail was the only other body part he could move, and it thumped weakly.

Mate, his wolf hummed, joyous in spite of the throbbing pain. *Nina. My mate.*

They'd both survived, and Hunter and Cruz were all right, too.

A shot of bile rose in his throat. Kramer was dead — good riddance — but so was Tammy. Boone took a deep breath, wishing those two had never come along and pushed things to the breaking point. He hadn't wished Tammy dead so much as he wished to erase her from his past. That would have been enough.

"Boone," Nina murmured, stroking him between his shoulder blades. The perfect spot to ease the troubles out of his mind — for now, at least. God knew he'd have hell to pay when Silas returned to Hawaii and demanded an explanation. But everything had turned out all right, hadn't it? Nina was okay, and the enemy hadn't stolen the Spirit Stone. Silas couldn't complain about *that.*

Boone eased his head back to the ground and closed his eyes. *Everything is okay. Everything is o—*

The earth rumbled, and an engine hummed over a bump in the driveway.

"Uh, Boone?" Nina's voice was alarmed.

He blinked, wondering what was with the red and blue lights flashing in his eyes.

Nina's warm body left his side as she rose to her feet. What was going on?

157

He caught a glimpse of a police car easing down the driveway, half hidden by the trees. Apparently, someone had heard the fight and reported it. At first, Boone's groggy mind pitied the officer who would have to file the report on this scene. But then it hit him, and he scrambled to his feet. Shifters had to protect the secret of their existence from humans at all costs. If they didn't, disaster could ensue. The couple of times in history that humans had discovered shifters had resulted in riotous hunts that had nearly driven his kind out of existence. Dragons had been decimated to a pitiful few. Entire wolf packs had been exterminated by angry mobs. Any surviving bear shifters had taken refuge in the mountains, and tigers — well, Cruz's family was the most recent example of the havoc humans could inflict.

Shit. He'd had a vague plan for calling in a couple of shifter friends to help erase evidence of the fight, but there was no time for that now.

Although it hurt like hell, he managed a quick shift back to human form. He was naked, but that would be easier to concoct a cover story for than explaining a wolf. Kramer and his mercenaries had shifted to human form shortly after taking their last breath as all shifters did, resuming their dominant forms. Cruz executed a lightning-fast shift, too, while Hunter had lumbered somewhere out of sight.

Boone limped over to the Jeep and pulled a pair of cargo pants out of the back.

"Good old Hunter, always prepared," Cruz muttered, grabbing a pair for himself.

Boone looked around. Where was Hunter? And how the hell was he going to explain all these bodies to the police?

"Now what?" Nina murmured when he stepped to her side.

His mind spun, trying to think up a plausible explanation. The car door squeaked open, and an officer jumped out, holding a gun.

"Freeze!"

Boone stuck his hands up, and Nina yelped. "Help!"

Help, he figured, was a good place to start.

"These men tried to kidnap me and... and... " Nina tried.

Boone stared at the cop. The sun was behind the squad car, but when he squinted, he could make out glossy black hair, soft features, and a feminine figure. Shit. Of all people, did it have to be her?

"Officer Meli," he groaned.

From the corner of his eye, Boone caught a hint of a movement, and he prayed Hunter was still out of sight. The bear half of his friend didn't like relinquishing control once it took command of Hunter's body. As a human, Hunter was a pussy cat. As a grizzly... Well, it was a good thing he was on Boone's side.

"No!" Nina screamed, spinning when she caught the motion, too.

"Freeze!" Officer Meli cried, turning her gun to the right.

Boone's weary mind was half a step behind. He looked on in horror as a wolf leaped at the policewoman — one last wolf they had assumed dead.

"Stop!" Boone yelled, though his legs buckled instead of running to intercept the foe.

Cruz's reaction time was slow, too, and Boone assumed the worst. Officer Meli would shoot the wolf, but a regular bullet wouldn't stop a shifter. It would tear her throat out before Boone could intervene.

The policewoman fired and took one shocked step backward, but the wolf raced on with Cruz and Boone two steps behind.

No, Boone wanted to scream. *No, no, no!*

A bird fluttered out of nowhere — an owl? — and slowed the wolf briefly, but not enough for Boone to catch the bastard. Then a roar split through the air, and a huge brown mass hurtled out from the right. A grizzly, terrifying to behold — even to Boone, who recognized Hunter, though he'd never, ever seen his friend move that fast. Hunter hammered forward, unsheathed his deadly claws, and tore into the wolf's haunches. The rogue screamed in pain as the grizzly fell over him.

Officer Meli stumbled back with wide, disbelieving eyes, and Cruz caught her hand just as she cocked the gun for a second shot. Boone raced up and blocked the view as Hunter finished the wolf off for good. Officer Meli didn't need to see that. He didn't particularly want to watch, either. His eyes stayed on the owl that circled once, then flew off, leaving Boone to wonder what that had been all about. He didn't have time to wonder for long, though, because a moment later, the area went deathly quiet.

Boone turned slowly. Hunter, still in bear form, backed away from the slain wolf. His mournful eyes fixed on the policewoman. He shook his fur, sat back on his haunches, and—

"Oh, shit," Boone murmured.

Hunter's bear half had taken over during the fight, but his human side pushed toward the surface at the sight of the woman he loved. He shifted in plain sight of Officer Meli and stood quietly, working his jaw.

The policewoman gasped, lowering her gun. "Hunter."

Boone bit his lip. In all the time Boone had known them, Office Meli and Hunter had always been painfully formal with each other, keeping their distance in spite of the obvious attraction that pulled them together again and again. Boone had never heard the policewoman use Hunter's first name. Not that she got much chance to since the bear rarely broke the speed limit, but she'd found a few clever excuses to pull him over from time to time. A broken taillight here, a quick check of inspection dates there — and Hunter had always glowed for days afterward.

Well, he sure wasn't glowing now. He just gulped and stared at her.

"Dawn..."

When Hunter took a step forward, the policewoman stepped back, and Hunter's face fell.

"Let me explain," Nina said, stepping up with her hands in clear view.

Boone whipped his head around. Nina had just found out about shifters herself. How was she going to explain? But her soft, feminine voice seemed like the only thing getting through to Officer Meli, so Boone held his tongue.

"They saved me," Nina said. "I was being kidnapped, but Hunter, Boone, and Cruz stopped them..." The words flowed off her tongue in a rapid stream.

"But he... he... " Officer Meli stuttered.

"He's Hunter," Nina said. "Just like Boone is Boone, and Cruz is Cruz."

Boone's heart swelled. God, did he love his mate.

The radio in the squad car squawked, making Office Meli jolt. "I have to report... "

Boone barely held back from cutting her off and raised his hands instead. "Please don't report this. Let us explain."

Officer Meli looked at Hunter, who murmured, "The wolf was going to kill you. I had to stop him... "

Boone was pretty sure the policewoman wasn't too worried about that part. It was the shifter part that made her turn pale. She stared and stared until the radio came alive again.

"I don't understand it all, either," Nina said when the cop turned toward her vehicle. "But one thing is clear to me, and I know it has to be clear to you. These aren't the bad guys, Officer. I owe them a chance to explain. You owe them a chance to explain. Please, let's hear them out."

The policewoman slowed but didn't stop, and Cruz glanced at Boone.

We have to stop her. She can't report this.

Boone shook his head quickly. Things were bad enough as they were. And anyway, Hunter wouldn't let either of them touch the woman he loved, even if it meant disaster for them all.

Everyone stared in silence as Officer Meli reached into the squad car and pulled the radio out. "Unit 239, checking in."

Boone went stiff all over as the dispatcher's staticky voice came through.

"Please," Hunter whispered, reaching a hand toward the policewoman.

Boone pulled Nina closer, wondering if he'd won over his mate only to lose her. If Officer Meli reported what she'd seen, half the Maui police force would swarm the place, and he and his shifter brothers would be... well, screwed.

Officer Meli pinched her lips, staring at Boone. His chin dropped in defeat as she opened her mouth to reply to the call.

"Negative," the policewoman murmured. "Negative," she repeated, making Hunter's head snap up. "False report. All units stand down."

If Nina hadn't been gripping his hand, Boone would have sat hard on his ass.

"Thank God," Nina murmured. "Thank God."

Chapter Nineteen

Three days later. . .

The cool water of the shower rushed over Nina's skin, and she closed her eyes to Boone's gentle touch. He slid the soap over her back, caressing every inch of her body. Gradually, he worked his way lower. . . lower. . .

Nina sighed and caught his hand. "We're supposed to be getting ready, Boone."

"I am getting ready," he rumbled into her ear. "Ready to love my mate all over again."

Her blood heated at the suggestion of even more pleasure at the hands of her lover. But they'd already spent most of the morning screwing, plus half the night.

Perfectly normal for a pair of freshly mated wolves, Boone had insisted, giving her a naughty grin. *The others will understand.*

The bite mark on Nina's neck tingled. The mark of the mating bite. She and Boone were bonded forever, and her whole soul rejoiced.

"Later, my love," she said, trying to slow him down with a kiss. It almost backfired, though, because his heat drew her in, and she started running her hands down his toned body all over again. She caught herself an inch away from his cock and stopped. "Bad wolf."

Boone put on a sad puppy-dog look, and she laughed.

"You're a very bad wolf, and I love you for it. But we really need to get moving. We can pick up where we stopped later."

Boone guided her hand back to his hips. "Promise me, my mate."

"I promise if you promise."

"I promise," he said, growing serious.

I promise to love and protect you forever, my mate, his wolf hummed into her mind.

Ever since the mating bite, she could hear every thought Boone sent her way. That was one more thing to get used to in her new life — a life she already loved. She had the world's best mate, and she got to live in a gorgeous little cottage by the sea. A tiny slice of paradise, and she never had to leave.

She gazed around as she dressed, counting her luck all over again. So much had happened to her, it was still hard to believe.

"Don't forget that," Boone said, tilting his head toward the ruby.

She'd pulled it out an hour earlier — before Boone had drawn her into another mind-blowing round of sex, that is — and left it on the bedside table, glowing in the sun beside her mother's teddy bear. When she took the gem in her fingers and held it up, it warmed her hand in a reassuring way, and a faint whisper reached her ears.

You have nothing to fear from me — you, the new keeper of the Firestone. My last keeper chose well.

Nina smiled at the memory of sweet old Lewis McGee and his note. *I wish you all the love, laughter, and joy that was in my dear wife's heart.*

Nina sighed. True love. Lewis McGee had been blessed by the ruby, though she doubted he'd known about its special powers. Now she was the one blessed by it.

With the ruby in one hand and Boone's warm grip in the other, Nina walked up the path, grateful for the strength both gave her. She'd known she would have to face Silas at some point, and this was it. According to Boone, Silas had returned late the previous night and immediately set a meeting time.

As in, right now.

Silas, the dragon. She took a deep breath. Everyone was gathering, and it scared her a little bit. The good news was a hot new celebrity scandal had broken out in Hollywood, and the press had dropped her story like a dead fish, so Silas hadn't returned to find a posse of reporters blocking the front gate. At least there was that.

The other good news was that Kai, Silas's cousin, and Kai's mate, Tessa, had returned to Hawaii two days before Silas did. Meeting Tessa was like reuniting with a long-lost friend, and the little time Nina spent away from Boone, she'd spent with Tessa having long, girl-to-girl talks. They'd laughed over each of the men's quirks, talked dirty about amazing shifter sex, and cried, too, sharing what they'd each been through. They'd also discovered that with a little effort, they could read each other's minds much like they could with their mates. It seemed like an incredible discovery, but Boone had just shrugged.

"Sure. You're part of the same pack."

He'd explained that, too. Wolf shifters usually lived in all-wolf packs. Bears lived in clans, dragons in weyrs, and tigers...

"Tigers keep to themselves," Boone had sighed, pointing in the direction of Cruz's house, all the way out at one end of the estate. Then he'd grinned and whispered, "If you want a good laugh, tell the others I said *pack*. We argue about what to call it all the time."

Nina had decided not to try that just yet. She was just happy to call the place home.

Tessa, a striking redhead with a warm smile, waved as Nina approached the meeting house.

Remember, they're just big puppies, she whispered into Nina's mind.

Nina pursed her lips, looking at the men gathered there. Tessa had also told her Koa was Hawaiian for an elite class of warriors, and that's what she saw in the men. Not a puppy among them. They were all big and battle-hardened, fiercely loyal and frighteningly powerful. Kai was the tall, dark-haired man pressed up to Tessa's side. Cruz paced along the perimeter of the building, restless as ever. Hunter hung back in the shadows, looking so pained, Nina wanted to give him a hug. It wasn't her touch he needed, though. Officer Meli had agreed to keep the shifter fight under wraps, but she'd left the scene looking wary and conflicted. When Hunter had tried to stop

165

her for a final word, she'd hurried away, and the grizzly hadn't smiled since.

Nina squeezed Boone's hand. Hunter had helped her earn her destined mate. Someday, somehow, she would figure out a way to do the same for the grizzly.

"Let's start," Silas said, pulling Nina back to the business at hand.

Silas was terrifying — tall and dark and sheer power. But when he moved through a beam of sunlight, Nina saw what she hadn't noticed at first: deep lines of worry creasing his brow, and fingers that tapped restlessly. According to Boone, Silas was in charge of the estate and the group of shifters who lived there. The responsibility had to be crushing.

Maybe he needs a hug, like Hunter, she half joked to Tessa.

Ha. I don't recommend you try it. But someday, you and I will find him a mate, too.

Nina grinned and gave Tessa a hidden thumbs-up.

"I don't know whether to be relieved or furious," Silas started, motioning everyone to the couches set in one section of the meeting house.

Relieved, Boone murmured into Nina's mind.

"I'm sorry," she said immediately. "I never meant to bring you trouble. . . "

Silas shook his head, and to Nina's surprise, the gesture was gentle, not curt. "Trouble has a way of finding us, it seems."

Everyone went quiet, and Nina saw Hunter close his eyes.

"You said the Spirit Stones would call to each other," Tessa said. "Is that what caused all this?"

The redhead stretched her arm out and opened her hand, setting a huge emerald on the table. Nina stared and slowly held her ruby up to the light, letting one facet after another catch and magnify the light. When she set it down next to the emerald, both gems glowed brighter, casting red and green shadows on the white tablecloth.

"Spirit Stones," Nina whispered, looking at Silas. Boone had explained the basics, but even he was stumped about the ruby.

"That is the Lifestone," Silas said in a reverent voice, pointing to Tessa's emerald. "It magnifies the bearer's innate powers." Then he gestured at the ruby. "Yours is the Firestone."

"What power does it have?" Boone asked. "I haven't been able to figure it out."

Every head turned to Silas, who nodded gravely. "Fire is power. Fire can be a boon, but it can destroy, too."

Nina shivered, remembering how Tamara had screamed and writhed.

"The Firestone reflects the bearer's qualities back on them. It seeks and rewards the pure." He paused, looking at Nina.

She dropped her eyes, feeling awfully self-conscious.

"And it punishes the evil," Silas finished.

Nina closed her eyes on the image of a dying Tamara.

"But a truly powerful shifter. . . " Kai murmured.

Silas nodded. "A truly strong shifter might be able to channel the power of the Firestone and use it for his own gain. To corrupt the good and ally with dark powers."

"Someone like Drax," Kai whispered.

Nina saw Tessa's eyes flicker with fear. Nina had heard about Drax — the most powerful dragon of all. An evil dragon that Silas had tangled with a long time ago.

"Does Drax know about the Firestone?" she asked, looking at Boone.

I will protect you forever, her lover's eyes promised.

She forced a smile. Boone had certainly proven himself with landborne shifters. But a dragon?

Tessa nudged her foot under the table. *Together, we are strong. Stronger than any of us could ever be alone. We're one weyr now.*

Nina couldn't hold back a faint smile, remembering Boone's comment about packs. She looked from one face to another, and they all bore the same determined expression. *Together, we are strong.*

Poor Boone — she was probably clutching his hand too hard, but Nina couldn't help it. For most of her life, it had been just her and her mother. She'd never had much of an extended family, either. But now, she did. She was part of that *we*. Slowly, Boone's mating bite would work on her and allow her to shift, and she made a quiet vow to learn everything she needed to protect her pack. Tessa was learning dragon fighting skills; Nina would do the same as a wolf. She didn't savor the thought of having to use such skills, but if it meant protecting her mate, her pack, her future kids—

Her breath caught as an image of Boone popped into her mind — Boone cooing at a tiny bundle wrapped in pink. No, wait. A blue bundle, too. Holy smokes. He held one in each arm.

She clutched the table. Did destiny have twins in store for her somewhere down the line?

A ray of light caught in the ruby, making it wink.

Nina took a deep breath. No need to think too far ahead. The present was good enough. And if ever evil visited again, she'd do her part to repel it.

Boone kissed her knuckles. *You and me. Side by side.*

She listened as the others murmured, considering the other Spirit Stones. But it was all too much for her overloaded mind, and she stood quickly. A cup of tea might help her settle down as the others discussed the long-lost treasure.

"The Waterstone..."

"The Windstone..."

"The Earthstone..."

The room grew quiet as everyone chewed on the notion.

"Coffee, anyone?" she asked, coming around with a pot. "Tea?" It might help them settle down, too.

Boone laughed and pulled her into his lap. "You know you don't have to waitress any more, right?"

She elbowed herself free carefully and poured tea into the cup Tessa pushed forward.

"I guess old habits die hard. I'll be pouring coffee forty years from now."

"Fine with me," Boone chuckled, his eyes bright with the thought of sharing so many years.

Nina grinned. In truth, she never wanted to give up the habit. She might not have to waitress for a living, thanks to Lewis McGee's incredible gift, but she'd never stop enjoying the way people smiled when she filled their mugs. Liquid sunshine, as her boss used to say.

Bringing joy to the world, one mugful at a time. That was the way Lewis put it.

She stepped over to Silas and poured him a coffee, black. She looped back to the kitchen, grabbed a jar, and continued to Hunter.

"Chamomile tea. Perfect with a little honey," she murmured.

Hunter looked up at her and managed a weak smile.

Nina sighed. Some people had a gift for music. Others, for languages. Hers was a simple gift, but it was enough. Even Cruz gave her an encouraging nod.

Silas swirled his coffee for a long time then sighed. "Back to business." He looked around, and Nina swore he was trying to look stern. But the edge was gone from his voice, and his eyes weren't quite as hard as before.

Keep that coffee coming, Tessa joked in a private aside. *I'll cook up some steak, and we'll have that beast tamed in no time.*

Nina didn't know about the *in no time* part, but maybe there was hope for Silas. Hunter, on the other hand. . .

"When we settled here at Koa Point," Silas said, addressing the other men, "we agreed to some ground rules. Number one: no humans."

Nina winced and wandered back to the kitchen.

"Humans? I don't see any humans," Boone growled.

Nina hid a grin. Technically, she was a shifter now, too. And weird as the prospect of changing into wolf form was, she couldn't wait to try it. Running on all fours beside Boone, singing at the full moon with him. . . Something deep in her soul yearned for it.

"I don't see any humans here, either," Kai grumbled, pulling Tessa closer.

Silas sighed. At first, Nina had assumed he'd be the barking-orders, autocratic type, but the respect he had for his men shone through.

"Seriously, I think we might have to revisit the no-humans policy," Boone said, looking at Hunter.

169

The bear looked sadder than ever and downed his tea in one gulp.

"No humans," Cruz growled. "Don't get me wrong. Tessa is okay. Nina, too."

Gee, thanks, Tessa sighed.

"But otherwise — no humans, I say. They're unpredictable. Irrational. Dangerous."

"Not all humans," Boone shot back. "Some are smart. Amazing. Wonderful."

Nina smiled a mile wide when her mate locked eyes with her.

"Hunter? What do you think?" Silas asked.

Hunter studied the bottom of his teacup, then shoved his chair back and stalked off, muttering something about catching up with work.

"May I make a suggestion?" Nina ventured in the awkward silence that ensued.

Silas waved his hand, telling her to go on.

"What about you take it on a case-by-case basis?" she said, careful to use the word *you*, putting the ball in his court. Inside, her heartstrings pulled a little. She'd once heard Lewis say that to one of the few friends he brought to the diner. *Take it on a case-by-case basis.*

"Makes sense to me," Kai said, nodding to Silas.

"Me, too," Boone said.

Cruz grumbled but didn't protest.

"Hmpf," Silas mumbled, not committing himself either way, and another heavy minute ticked by.

"So, Nina," Tessa said, chopping into the silence in a clear attempt to lighten things up. "Did you talk to the lawyer about your donation yet?"

"I'm waiting to hear about the details," she said.

"Lawyers," Boone growled. "He's probably just taking longer so he can charge more."

Nina swatted at his back. "He said he'd do it *pro bono.*"

"Twenty-five million," Boone shook his head, but she caught the veiled pride in his voice. "Giving half of your money away."

"Half of Lewis's money," she corrected him.

"Your money," Boone tried, then pointed at the ruby and sighed. "Figures I'd find me a mate who's pure of heart."

"Yeah, go figure," Kai ribbed.

Nina laughed. In truth, Boone had loved the idea the second she mentioned it — donating half the money to a women's cancer prevention program. Nina was sure Lewis would have approved, and twenty-five million still seemed like plenty of money to keep. The only thing she'd decided to spend it on so far was tuition at the state college so she could finally earn her psychology degree. Classes didn't start for another six weeks, so she had time to settle into her new life.

"Are we done?" Boone asked Silas far too sweetly.

"For now," Silas growled, shooting Boone a *Watch it, buster* look.

"Good. Because my mate and I have pressing business at the beach."

Nina blushed. From the way Boone ran his hand down her back, it was pretty clear what kind of *business* he meant. But she, too, felt the pull, the insistent need.

Perfectly normal for a pair of freshly mated wolves, Boone said with a sly grin, pulling her from the table.

"Don't forget the ruby," Tessa said, giving her own mate a heated, *Don't you and I also have pressing business?* look.

Nina took the gem and scurried away with Boone. The second they turned the first corner of the path, he pulled her into a huge, back-bending Hollywood kiss.

"Always wanted to do that," he grinned, hauling her upright again.

"Me, too," she joked, pretending to lean him into the reverse position. "If you hold the ruby for me, I think I might even manage it."

Boone threw his hands up. "Whoa. No way. I'm thinking way too many impure thoughts right now to risk touching it."

Nina pocketed the gem and sidled closer to him, giggling. "Oh, yes? What kind of thoughts?"

"Thoughts of you naked on our bed."

Our bed. She loved how quickly his home had become their home, how easily she slipped into his life.

"And where are you while I'm naked on our bed?" she asked, kissing the line of his jaw.

"Inside you," he said, all husky with need. "My mate."

Her inner thermostat rocketed right off the charts, and she wrapped a leg around his side, craving the contact. But Boone went all serious again, gazing into her eyes. "Thank you," he whispered.

She laughed. "For what?"

He waved a hand as if he didn't know where to start. "For everything. I love you, Nina."

He threaded his fingers through her hair and planted a sweet, soft kiss on her lips. A kiss she hijacked a few seconds later when the carnal need became too much to bear. Her tongue swept over his, and her nipples peaked against his chest.

Then she pulled back, panting. "Now take me home and show me you're not all bark and no bite, wolf."

Boone laughed and ran his hands down her back. "Be careful what you wish for, my mate."

Sneak Peek: Lure of the Bear

Aloha Shifters: Jewels of the Heart, Book 3

There's not much that can get this grizzly shifter worked up — except a threat to the woman he has secretly loved for years. Then all bets are off, and he's willing to risk anything — including the most closely guarded secret of his lonely shifter soul.

* * *

A beep sounded, making everyone at the Kapa'akea resort look up, and Hunter caught a flash of red racing in from the main road.

"Him again," the security guard muttered at the sight of Boone zipping up in the Ferrari.

The wolf shifter flashed one of his winning grins as he pulled up. "Hop in."

"Hop?" Hunter sighed as he squeezed into the low-slung car. "Couldn't you have driven the Land Rover?"

"No time to waste," Boone said as he raced back to the highway and made the left turn for home. "My errands took forever. I need to get back to my mate and—" He cut himself off there. "Oh. I mean. . . "

Hunter looked at his feet as an awkward silence fell over the car — silence broken a few minutes later when the car swerved, and another beeped.

"Oops," Boone murmured, unfazed.

"Keep your eyes on the road," Hunter muttered as the Ferrari's speed inched up.

"No problem." Boone shrugged, jerking the wheel to straighten out.

"You need to slow down, too."

"Nah. Like I said, no time to waste."

Hunter braced his arms on the dashboard as the scenery flashed by. "Boone..."

"I got this, man. We're nearly there."

They were nearly to the curve staked out by Officer Dawn Meli off the Maui Police, too. If she was on duty, she was bound to pull them over, and Hunter wasn't ready to face her yet.

"Boone..."

"Live a little, man," Boone said, racing around the corner.

Hunter peeked right, and his heart pounded at the sight of Dawn's white-and-blue cruiser.

She's back! his bear practically leaped for joy. *She's back! Maybe she'll pull us over.*

The Ferrari raced on, and Hunter kept his eyes glued to the side mirror, waiting for the flash of police lights.

"Hey," Boone murmured, slowing down. "She's not pulling me over?"

The joy that had burst into Hunter's soul slowly seeped out. Dawn wasn't pulling them over. She was avoiding him, just as he'd been avoiding her ever since the shifter battle that had revealed his animal side.

Boone slowed even more, then signaled a left turn into a private drive.

Hunter made a face. "Wait. What are you doing? This isn't the driveway to Koa Point."

Boone put the Ferrari into reverse, scattering gravel as he headed back the way they'd come. "I'm going back."

Hunter dug his nails into the dashboard. "Whoa. What?"

"I have a right be pulled over, damn it," Boone said with a sly look on his face.

"I thought you were in a rush to get back to your mate."

"I am, but this is important, too."

174

"Boone," Hunter growled, to no avail. He sank as low in his seat as he could when Boone drove past the squad car again, but damn it, the Ferrari didn't offer much space to hide a bear shifter of his size. "Don't do this, Boone."

"Time to man up, bear." Boone chuckled as he turned the car yet again. He drove right up to the pullout and parked next to the squad car, putting Hunter window-to-window with a wide-eyed Officer Meli.

His breath caught, and his blood warmed.

Mate, his bear hummed. *My perfect mate.*

She was perfect in every possible way. Her fine features, her glossy black hair, her dark, searching eyes. Back in high school, there'd been people who talked about Dawn getting modeling contracts and hitting it big thanks to her gorgeous blend of Polynesian, Asian, and Caucasian features, but she'd shunned the suggestion and gone to law school instead. And after law school, she'd surprised everyone — again — by going into law enforcement.

My mate always does the unexpected, his bear said with a dreamy sigh.

"Officer Meli!" Boone called cheerily.

Hunter closed his eyes, savoring a whiff of her flowery scent.

"Mr. Hawthorne," she said in an icy voice that warmed and wavered when she looked at Hunter. "Mr. Bjornvold."

Hunter snapped his eyes open again. "Dawn," he whispered.

"You didn't pull me over," Boone said.

"No, I didn't." Her dark eyes were hard and unamused, but when they strayed toward Hunter, they flickered — and not in fear. More like... recognition. Maybe even warmth.

I told you! his bear cried. *I told you she loves us.*

But why would she? Humans didn't know about destined mates.

Deep inside, our mate knows, his bear insisted. *Destiny told her, too.*

"I was speeding," Boone said.

Officer Meli's brow furrowed. "I decided to let it go this once."

"But speeding is unlawful. I really think you ought to give me a ticket."

She pushed the door of her squad car open and stood with her hands on her hips. "Mr. Hawthorne," she said in a stern, policewoman's voice. "I decide when I issue a ticket, is that clear?"

How she managed to look beautiful and menacing at the same time, Hunter didn't know.

She'd make a great bear, his inner beast sighed.

"Yes, ma'am," Boone said, putting on his best chagrined schoolboy look as he swung the car door open.

Officer Meli went into a defensive stance, one arm hovering over the weapon at her hip. "Hold it right there."

Boone stood and stretched. "Sorry. An old army injury is suddenly flaring up. I need to walk it off."

Hunter furrowed his brow. Boone had his share of war wounds, as had every member of their Special Forces unit. But as a quick-healing shifter, Boone didn't suffer any long-term effects. What was he up to?

Old army what? Hunter demanded, stepping out of the car at the same moment Dawn asked, "Old army injury?" She arched her perfect eyebrows, then spun to face Hunter. "Whoa. You hold it, too."

Hunter threw his hands up as Boone faked a grimace and limped up the dirt track that led from the pullout point toward the West Maui mountains. "I'll be fine in a few minutes. Don't worry."

"Worry?" Dawn muttered, not sounding the least concerned. Her eyes darted from Boone's back to Hunter's face.

Hunter pushed the car door closed and leaned against it, keeping his hands in plain view. Damn. What had he been thinking, hopping out of the car like that?

I was thinking, get closer to my mate, his bear murmured inside.

We'll scare her, he hissed back.

Boone's footsteps crunched over gravel, then faded into the distance, leaving Hunter alone with Dawn. He scrubbed a hand over his jaw, wondering what to do.

Time to man up, you stupid bear. Boone's words echoed through his mind, and a few awkward seconds later, he finally spoke. "Look— "

"Look," Dawn said at exactly the same time.

They both stopped cold, looking at each other.

Hunter scuffed the dirt with his boot. "Ladies first."

"No, you first," she insisted, crossing her arms.

Right. If only he knew what to say other than, *Look.*

Say I love you, his bear tried.

Hunter shook his head. No way was he opening with that line.

Say, you can trust me.

Hunter shoved his hands deeper into his pockets. Damn it, why was it that a bear who didn't fear anything had to be so scared of uttering a few words?

Then kiss her.

He gritted his teeth. Much as he'd like to, that wouldn't work, either.

She sighed. "Tongue-tied as ever, I see."

Hunter looked up. Another woman might have laced the words with scorn, but not Dawn. If anything, there was a hint of fondness in her voice. Or was he imagining things?

They stood facing each other for a full minute, speechless. Any second, Hunter figured, his brief stint in heaven would be over — just being close to Dawn was heaven — so he imprinted the moment into his mind. A wisp of hair had strayed out of her single braid, and the sea breeze twirled it exactly the way he fantasized about doing himself. The sun shone from high overhead, casting her face into smooth fields of shadow and light. When her eyes strayed to his chest and back to his eyes, her throat bobbed with a tiny swallow.

Hunter gulped, too, because it was happening again. That magical aura that overwhelmed him every time he came close to his mate. The sensation that rose out of nowhere and wound around the two of them, locking the outside world away. The hum of passing cars, the scratch of insects in the surrounding scrub — all sound faded until the only thing Hunter heard was the beat of his heart. All he saw was the faint rise and fall of

177

Dawn's shoulders with each deep breath. Her face was bright and clear, but everything else was blurry, as if the sun was slowly turning a lens and focusing all its light on her.

This is your mate, a whisper came from somewhere deep in the earth. *This is your destiny.*

Dawn's eyes shone brighter than ever, and she leaned forward slightly.

She needs you as much as you need her, the voice said, coaxing him along.

A yellow butterfly fluttered between them, but even that was a blur. Nothing mattered but Dawn.

His lips moved with words he couldn't form, and when his hand brushed hers, she didn't jerk away.

"Hunter," she whispered.

* * *

That's just a little taste of another unforgettable paranormal romance! Get your own copy of *Lure of the Bear* to follow all the suspense, emotion, and romance!

Books by Anna Lowe

Aloha Shifters - Jewels of the Heart

Lure of the Dragon (Book 1)

Lure of the Wolf (Book 2)

Lure of the Bear (Book 3)

Lure of the Tiger (Book 4)

Love of the Dragon (Book 5)

The Wolves of Twin Moon Ranch

Desert Hunt (the Prequel)

Desert Moon (Book 1)

Desert Wolf: Complete Collection (Four short stories)

Desert Blood (Book 2)

Desert Fate (Book 3)

Desert Heart (Book 4)

Desert Yule (a short story)

Desert Rose (Book 5)

Desert Roots (Book 6)

Sasquatch Surprise (a Twin Moon spin-off story)

Blue Moon Saloon

Perfection (a short story prequel)

Damnation (Book 1)

Temptation (Book 2)

Redemption (Book 3)

Salvation (Book 4)

Deception (Book 5)

Celebration (a holiday treat)

Shifters in Vegas

Paranormal romance with a zany twist

Gambling on Trouble

Gambling on Her Dragon

Gambling on Her Bear

Serendipity Adventure Romance

Off the Charts

Uncharted

Entangled

Windswept

Adrift

Travel Romance

Veiled Fantasies

Island Fantasies

visit www.annalowebooks.com

Free Books

Get your free e-books now!

Sign up for my newsletter at *annalowebooks.com* to get three free books!

- *Desert Wolf*: Friend or Foe (Book 1.1 in the Twin Moon Ranch series)

- *Off the Charts* (the prequel to the Serendipity Adventure series)

- *Perfection* (the prequel to the Blue Moon Saloon series)

About the Author

USA Today and Amazon bestselling author Anna Lowe loves putting the "hero" back into heroine and letting location ignite a passionate romance. She likes a heroine who is independent, intelligent, and imperfect – a woman who is doing just fine on her own. But give the heroine a good man – not to mention a chance to overcome her own inhibitions – and she'll never turn down the chance for adventure, nor shy away from danger.

Anna loves dogs, sports, and travel – and letting those inspire her fiction. On any given weekend, you might find her hiking in the mountains or hunched over her laptop, working on her latest story. Either way, the day will end with a chunk of dark chocolate and a good read.

Visit AnnaLoweBooks.com

Made in the USA
Coppell, TX
29 November 2020